Incantations of Blood

Savannah R. Fischer

Book Cover by Ruth Anna Evans

Edited by Stephanie Huddle

1st edition 2024

Praise for Incantations of Blood

"In Incantations of Blood, Fischer delivers a gripping tale of supernatural terror that keeps you on the edge of your seat. The eerie atmosphere and relentless suspense make this a standout in the horror genre. Prepare to be utterly captivated." --Steven Pajak, Author of THE DEVIL'S DOORWAY

"[Fischer] has killed it with her impressive debut novel Incantations of Blood. She takes a premise that is both comfortably familiar and exhilarating in its fresh take, and infuses the struggles of grief and loss with elements of the occult and dark small town secrets. I only expect great things from this new author. --Megan Stockton, Author of LOVLEY DARK & DEEP

"Incantations is a bold debut. Fischer proves she has the deft abilities of a veteran author, unafraid to explore the darkest aspects of horror. When you finish this novel, you'll be as changed as the residents of Shady Grove, and a piece of it's demonic underground will stick with you." --Gage Greenwood, Author of ON A CLEAR DAY YOU CAN SEE BLOCK ISLAND

"A debut has never gripped me the way this one has. Fischer is a force to be reckoned with this masterfully crafted mosaic of the macabre. The way she bobs and weaves in and out of scenes, it's as if she's sitting with the reader on a rollercoaster ride through Shady Grove. My interest was piqued from the prologue and she had a chokehold on my attention throughout!"--K.L. Allister, Author of THE WILLOWS

Also By

Table of Contents

Prologue: In a Forest Dark and Deep

Celia crept through the murky forest; her once-white tennis shoes turned the color of discarded coffee grounds as a dense layer of muck adhered to the canvas. Leaves and broken twigs, sticking out at odd angles, tousled her blonde hair as she continued toward her goal. Her GPS had been her steady guide, its soothing voice shepherding her in the right direction as she navigated around the dense foliage.

Using her phone as a flashlight, she kept careful watch for hazards. Scrapes stung her ravaged hands while blood oozed from her torn knee beneath her shredded jeans from the hard fall she had taken earlier. There was no path, but she knew the direction she needed to go. The strange text she received had promised her critical information in exchange for a clandestine meeting at the coordinates listed. As a reporter, she had heard of sources going to ungodly lengths to preserve their anonymity, but this was turning out to be a bit much. Her usual stories were fluff pieces for the local paper. No one knew she was investigating a series of seemingly unrelated disappearances in her free time. *They probably chose me since I'm not much of a threat. I'm just a baby journalist.* Still, if this source had information on Tayla Whittmer, the twenty-year-old woman who went missing in 2020, Celia needed to do whatever it took to get it. The Whittmer family deserved answers.

The usual scents of nature had given way to something else. Gone were the traces of crisp fallen leaves, damp earth, and fresh air. Something foul, almost sulfuric, replaced those usual scents. As the smell intensified, she knew she was getting close to its source. The stench of decomposition hung thick in the air; something was rotten in the forest's core. She couldn't fathom what could be causing the foul odor. The stink assaulted her senses, causing her eyes to water. She attempted to breathe through her mouth, but the onslaught of a bitter, acrid taste coated her tongue. Sputtering, Celia decided the smell was the better of the two options. She breathed shallowly in an attempt to avoid it as much as possible. Her focus broke when the GPS chirped, "You have reached your destination."

She paused, using the beam on her phone to take in her surroundings, but the shadows swallowed the wavering ray of light. She cursed herself for not bringing a more powerful flashlight or even a headlamp. The unexpected text had thrown her for a loop. *I got too excited...bloody fool.* Without her usual gear, she would pay the price for rushing off in a hurry. The foul odor was overpowering, and there seemed to be an ominous tension in the air. At first, only the trees were illuminated, shimmering with an otherworldly quality in the dim light. Celia gasped as her beam highlighted a mysterious shape lying on the ground next to a murky, miry pool. She approached cautiously, realizing as she got closer that the shape was an unmoving human form. She took a moment to assess the situation.

Listening intently, she took in the sounds of the forest. Somewhere in the distance, an owl hooted. She could hear the scurrying of tiny feet, probably a rodent hiding from predators. The only abnormalities were the stench, the foul black pool, and the shadowy silhouette near her feet. She knelt, taking extreme caution not to disturb the scene more than she already had. She gently grasped the wrist, desperately hoping to find a pulse. There was none. The corpse was still warm to the touch, meaning death occurred less than twelve hours ago.

She released the wrist and used her meager light to take in what details she could. The body belonged to a woman, her mouth open as if gasping for air. She noticed the petechiae in the eyes and the large fingerprints circling her neck. The woman was none other than Amanda Corey, a missing hitchhiker who was featured on the news just this morning. Celia stood up, instantly on high alert. *Oh no!* A quick pat down of her body revealed to her she had made a grave error; both her pepper spray and her stun gun were still in the glove box of her car. Amanda's prone form screamed danger. Celia's eyes kept flitting back to the strangulation marks, her eyes wide with fright. The GPS coordinates given to Celia led her right to the location of Amanda's final resting place. *Shit! I'm not safe here!!*

Her body broke out in a cold sweat. She no longer believed this to be a clandestine meeting. The danger glared at her in stark reality. *A setup!* She fell for an elaborate ruse to get her alone in the dank, dark woods. Her only goal now was to survive. She took a picture of the corpse so she could report it to the police when she got back to town. She refused to think in ifs. She would make it back home; she had to.

She became acutely aware that the previous sounds of forest animals had fallen silent. Wind whipped through the trees, startling her. The sound of rustling in the underbrush set her nerves ablaze. Something was heading in her direction. It was large, seemingly coming toward her exact location. As the panic set in, her mind whirled with the dangerous possibilities. It could be a pack of wild wolves, fur matted with blood while they foamed at the mouth, ready to tear her to shreds. Bobcats were a possibility too, their glowing eyes stalking her in the dark, waiting for the perfect moment to pounce at her throat. This deep in the woods, it could even be a bear. She could see it now, an unparalleled mass of black fur and hulking muscle lumbering toward her, ready to maul her. Would she still be alive when it cracked her open to eat her insides like honey from a hive? She gulped with fear, her breath catching in her throat. The not knowing was becoming unbearable. *Wait...what if it's a person?* She couldn't decide if that thought was comforting or not. A person could potentially be reasoned with, but considering there was already one dead body here, she didn't like her chances.

The sounds of whatever was approaching unnerved her, as if it wanted her to hear it. The rustling came closer, but she noted the absence of the sound of crunching leaves or snapping branches. Whatever was coming, it was moving slowly and deliberately. *This is it*, she thought. *Whoever lured me out here is going to kill me.*

Her skin prickled with unease as she heard the predator slow, then stop. Using her phone, she tried to survey the area, but even squinting, all she made out were dark shadows and trees. Every nerve in her body fired at her to run as the disquiet gave way to a real sense of danger. She cursed herself for leaving her defensive measures behind. *Stupid. Stupid. STUPID!* She knew better. It was dangerous for a lone woman at night in general, let alone in the middle of the woods. *Why didn't I tell Mom where I was going? No one knows I'm here!* The rustling stopped. Everything was quiet, the air thick with anticipation. Her pulse quickened as she felt eyes on her, and nature itself wanted to know what would happen next.

A branch snapped just a few feet behind her. The fine hairs on the back of her neck stood at attention as hot breath hit the sensitive area. She whirled, her eyes widening as she faced her worst fear. This wasn't a wild animal, but instead, the most dangerous predator on earth: a man. She attempted to catch a glimpse of her attacker's face. "Hello Celia," a deep voice whispered menacingly. *I know that voice!*

Her eyes filled with fright as a gloved hand thrust toward her throat. She recoiled, dodging his grasp by a fraction of an inch as she stepped back into the muck. "Ah ah ah, I wouldn't do that if I were you. There are more dangerous things than me in this forest." He knocked her phone from her hand, sending it clattering to the ground. He clutched at Celia's throat again as he kicked her phone into the pool. His large hand wrapped around her, squeezing and restricting the precious oxygen from reaching her lungs. Celia flailed, her desperate fingers raking at his face. Her nails found purchase on his skin, loosing rivulets of blood as they tore his fragile flesh. He let out a deep, barking laugh laced with menace. *No! This can't be happening. He knows me! Why is he trying to hurt me... unless? No!* Her brain spun as she fought for her life. She matched his kicks and punches blow for blow. Adrenaline pulsed through her veins as the battle progressed.

She kicked his shin with all her might and he inexplicably let go. "Have it your way," he grumbled. In disbelief, she took another step back. Her shoe sank impossibly deep as it squelched into the obsidian goo. Her assailant grinned wickedly, shoving her off balance. Her eyes widened as she fell. Shock registered on her face when she realized the man had played her all along, pushing her consistently backward to the edge of the pool. The noxious sludge encompassed her body, taking purchase wherever it could. The man stood, amusement etched on his dark features.

"H–hh–help me," she spluttered as the impossibly thick fluid flowed into her mouth, clogging her throat. The man stood there impassively as Celia thrashed wildly. Her hands scrambled for anything that could help pull her to safety, but to no avail. The glimpse she saw earlier had hidden the true nature of the pool of black filth, and it was determined to claim her. *I'm so sorry Mom... Dad. I should've been more careful.* Thick tendrils of muck coated her, sinking and drowning into the depths, until, in the blink of an eye, the pool swallowed her whole, a smattering of bubbles and ripples on the surface the only sign of a recent disturbance. The ooze was alive, and it wanted its due; this sacrifice would suffice. For now. The man kept vigil until the last bubbles disappeared from the pitch-black surface. He heaved the body of his previous victim into the murk, watching as it sank to its tomb with Celia. "Welcome to the lagoon Celia. It's been waiting for you, you nosey bitch," he sneered. As the pit feasted, the wounds on the man's face healed, a testament to the power of the ritual. Satisfied, he turned on his heel and began his methodical retreat back to civilization. A deep, booming disembodied laugh rumbled through the forest as the lagoon eagerly accepted its latest sacrifices.

Anne Dickenson awoke with a start at midnight, an unexplainable wave of anxiety making her heart rate spike. Something was horribly wrong; she just knew it. Her heart hammered in her chest. Her worst fears unfurled before her eyes when she found her daughter's bed still made, evidence Celia had not come home. She checked her phone, but the absence of missed calls or texts informing her that Celia wouldn't be back further cemented her mother's intuition. Her internal alarms blasted like the bass at the rock shows of her youth, shaking her to her core. *Something's wrong. Something's wrong. Something's WRONG!* She went to the living room, where she frantically called and texted her daughter for hours. Calls went straight to voicemail. Texts remained unread. The panic deepened with every creeping tick of the clock. As the hour chimed 5:00 am, Anne couldn't take the stress for one more minute. She dashed upstairs, desperately shaking her husband awake. "Ed! Ed! Wake up!"

"What, Anne?" he answered groggily.

"Have you heard from Celia?"

"Honey, it's 5:00 am. Maybe she went out early chasing a story?"

"No Ed. She hasn't been home at all. Her car isn't in the driveway, her phone is off, and there are no calls or texts saying not to expect her."

Ed sat up. This was very unlike Celia. She may be a twenty-two-year-old woman, but she still lived with them. Her job as a reporter for the local paper had her occasionally working strange hours, but she always let them know. She knew her parents worried.

"So her location tracking is off, but it looks like the last blip was Shady Grove Forest last night." Ed looked at his wife, his brow furrowing. Panic was written all over her face. "Maybe we should call the police, just to be safe." He hesitated, his paternal worry dueling with his usual calm nature. Did this warrant bothering the chief this early in the morning? Anne had no such qualms. Everyone knows the first seventy-two hours are the most important for missing person cases. She picked up her own phone and made the call, trying not to think about how many times she tried and failed to contact her daughter over the last few hours.

Her call led a couple of officers to the house, who grew more concerned as another unit reported there was no trace of Celia's car by the forest. The force roared into action, a perk of the Dickensons' close friendship with the chief. But despite the police's best efforts, it appeared Celia had vanished without a trace. Days turned to weeks as the town waited with bated breath for news of the missing woman. The police stopped short of linking the Celia Dickenson case with that of Amanda Corey, but the public was sure they had to be connected. Could a serial predator be on the loose?

September gave way to October, and before they knew it, Celia had missed Halloween and Thanksgiving.

As Christmas approached, Ed and Anne grew desperate. They called on a renowned medium by the name of Minerva Penderghast, whom they found online. Minerva had aided numerous investigations before, although always in an unofficial capacity. Her successful career had helped with the location of several missing persons, both dead and alive. She agreed to conduct a seance at the Dickenson's home.

On a blustery Christmas Eve night, she arrived. Anne watched, entranced, as the woman's turban tinkled with clinking coins as she moved in her long, flowing robe. Ed and Anne had prepared the dining room to her specifications, opening all the windows and cleansing the space with sage smoke. As the medium entered the room, Ed turned off the lights. The special candles she had sent dripped spice-scented wax as their flames danced around the heart of the home. Together, they ushered her toward the table.

Anne wrung her hands, a nervous habit she had picked up since the disappearance. "Thank you so much for coming. We've just been beside ourselves."

"Yes, please, anything you can do to help bring our daughter home. The house is so empty without her, I..."

Ed choked up. Anne clasped his hand. She knew he had put on a brave face to the world, but they both were heartbroken. They just wanted Celia back.

"Of course. I have a daughter myself; she'll be nineteen in the spring. My heart aches for you both. I will do my best to help get answers from the spirit world."

With an air of gravitas, Minerva sat down at the head of the table. She grasped the hands of the grieving parents and gave them instructions. "Remember, no matter what happens, do not let go of my hands. The spirit world holds more than just gentle souls seeking to connect with the mortal plane. It is our sacred duty to ensure nothing passes over to the barrier and into the land of the living."

Minerva drew a deep breath and began. "Spirits, I humbly call upon thee. Hear my cry! If Celia Dickenson is among you, answer me!" A decorative plate fell from the china cabinet, shattering, its jagged edges glinting in the candlelight.

"Something's here," whispered a frightened Anne. Minerva jerked, almost severing the circle, before Ed clamped down tightly on her hand. Her eyes glassed over as she focused on one of the wavering candles.

"Ed..." Anne was nervous now. *What are we doing? Can this woman really help find Celia?*

"Your daughter is neither among the living nor the dead. She is stuck in between, her location hidden from me. Dark forces are at play here. Something sinister is interfering with my sight."

"What does that mean?" cried out a shaking Anne, terror piercing her heart like a knife, cutting her to the core. Ed squeezed her hand, offering what meager comfort he could.

Minerva gasped as the interfering entity came into her field of vision. Suddenly, her eyes rolled back in her head, her body shaking with forceful convulsions. She opened her mouth, issuing forth a foul-smelling black substance. She choked on the thick sludge, splattering it upon the table in clotted shimmering droplets. A deep, malevolent voice boomed from Minerva. "Celia belongs to me now. Hold no illusions. She is gone from the mortal plane." The medium frothed at the mouth as she continued to shake. Without warning, she released the Dickensons' hands with a startled cry. The circle was broken.

The effect was immediate. The candles snuffed out, plunging the room into a shadowy gloom. Plates flew from the china cabinet, shattering upon the floor into a heap of razor-sharp pieces. Invisible hands slung the pieces through the air, slicing Anne across the arms and face. She cowered in her chair, the fright almost too much for her fragile heart. The temperature chilled, and puffs of breath lingered, barely visible, in the bitter cold. Minerva cried out, "Who are you? Ahhh-" she cut off.

"Anne!" Ed pushed back from the table, desperate to reach his wife.

Disembodied malicious laughter permeated the frigid air, surrounding the table and chilling the Dickensons to their cores. The laughter taunted them mercilessly as it changed directions, sweeping around the room so that it seemed to come from everywhere and nowhere all at once. Through the darkness, Ed groped for his wife's hand. He could barely make out a hulking figure lurking in the shadows. Enshrouded as it was, he could not see any details, but the ominous aura emanating from it was unmistakable. The smell of brimstone assaulted the trio, as demonic fire illuminated the room. Anne cried out in primal fear. Ed raised his arms as the figure came into view, just before something sharp plunged into his chest.

Anne screamed, believing her husband was dying as blood spurted from his gaping wound.

"Ed! Don't leave me, Ed. Please..."

The vicious laughter multiplied, coming from at least two voices. Anne closed her eyes and sobbed. Her husband was bleeding out before her. Beside her, she could hear the foul creatures attacking the medium. Something was tearing into her flesh, ripping and chewing in rapid succession. *That poor woman, she was only trying to help us. Oh Ed, please don't leave me all alone. I love you. I need you. Ed!*

"Begone, creatures of hell!" shouted an unexpected voice. The laughter turned into taunts as a small woman came into view. She began chanting in a foreign language, standing her ground, as she threw holy water in their direction. The creatures screeched in pain before disappearing in a cloud of acrid smoke. The strange, small woman had successfully banished the evil spirits back from whence they came.

As quickly as it had started, the ordeal was over. The vengeful laughter fell silent. The room plunged back into darkness as the spirits retreated, taking their hellfire with them. Nothing more crashed down from the china cabinet. The silence brought with it uncertainty after the brutal assault. *Is it really over?* Anne sighed with relief when a small cough shattered the quiet. Ed coughed again, his breathing slow and shallow. "Stay with me, Ed. We're going to get you some help." He answered with a low groan of pain, a further sign of life.

The unknown woman found the light switch. Anne turned toward the medium. She let out a blood-curdling shriek at the sight before her. At the head of the table, foam and black sludge coating her lips and dribbling down her chin, slumped the desecrated remains of Minerva Penderghast. Long ragged gashes trailed down her back; the flesh scored so deep in places that muscle and bone glistened with blood. Minerva bordered on decapitation, a large bite having removed most of her throat. Her vertebrae shined in the harsh overhead light. The wounds wept more of the same black substance that coated her mouth and the dining room table.

Ed lay on the floor; a vast wound through his chest and back pulsed more ichor with every beat of his heart. His breathing grew erratic as the pain and blood loss took hold. "Call the police while I tend to him," commanded the newcomer. Anne rose on shaking legs to call 911.

She held her husband's hand as the stranger spread herbs across his wound. "This should purify whatever poison there may be."

"Poison?"

"Demons always like to leave their victims with a little reminder of their encounter. Your husband is lucky the blow missed his heart." Anne fainted at the mention of demons. When the police arrived, they found a bloody scene including a dead woman, a man with an inexplicable chest wound, and a woman with multiple shallow lacerations who had fainted. No sign of the mystery woman was found, even though upon regaining consciousness, Anne made sure to credit her with saving their lives. She swore she knew her, but the terrifying events had fractured her memory, obscuring the woman's face. *Whoever you are, wherever you are, thank you. We owe you our lives.*

Meanwhile, deep in the forest of Shady Grove, hidden among the densely populated beech trees, a black heart lies, waiting to strike at its next innocent victim.

Chapter One: Welcome to Shady Grove

This town is nothing to look at, Maeve thought to herself as she gazed out at the city unfolding from the bus window. What appeared to be the main street ran east to west through the center and was dotted with various businesses and eateries. Streets full of houses branched off, running north and south. She contemplated the circumstances that had brought her here while absentmindedly stroking the pendant around her neck. Once the coroner released her mother's remains, Maeve opted for cremation. Following her mother's wishes, the ashes were scattered near the grounds of the Indiana Central State Hospital, supposedly one of the state's most haunted locations. She didn't quite understand her mother's affinity for the place. Minerva always just muttered that she hoped that even in death, she could help others cross over and find their eternal rest. A small portion of the ashes resided in the necklace, swirled into a mesmerizing array of stars against a blue background. It was made to resemble Van Gogh's The Starry Night, her mother's favorite painting. Minerva said it represented a world where the spirits were at peace, whatever that meant. The pendant served as a grounding tool, as well as a constant reminder of all Maeve had lost.

Her trek to Shady Grove began and ended with the Celia Dickenson case. Her mother came here to help but instead lost her life to some malevolent force in brutal fashion. The coroner only let her see the body with the sheet covering everything up to her mother's chin. "You don't want to see past that, Honey," he insisted. But still, she knew all the grisly details. Near decapitation. Lacerations. Black ichor. All things completely unexplainable in this world. It had been all over the papers and the internet. Most people thought it was a hoax, but Maeve knew the harsh reality. Science held no answers for her broken heart, but that didn't make it hurt any less. Grief was a burden she was forced to carry, like an iron weight buried in her chest. She would never be a carefree teenager again.

Maeve lost herself when she lost Minerva. All through life, they only had one another. At the tender age of eighteen, she had not been anywhere near ready to live in a world her mother did not also inhabit. She was cut loose, all alone in the great big world. How she longed for just a minuscule portion of her mother's abilities so she could attempt to contact her. Alas, she remained cut off from the veil, stuck firmly within the harsh confines of what Minerva claimed the spirits call the mortal plane. She suffered through Christmas, New Year's, even her birthday, horribly alone. Maeve felt unmoored without her mother's anchoring presence.

Without any sense of direction in life, Maeve decided to follow in her mother's footsteps. She hopped on a 3:25 am Greyhound bound for Shady Grove from Kalamazoo, MI, a nine-hour journey including a transfer in Chicago mid-route. The dark of the moonless night shrouded most of the scenery, but as they entered Indiana, the melodic swaying of cornfields became unmistakable. It was beautiful and eerie, as if a ghost breathed upon the stalks, making them sway rhythmically. *In. Out. In. Out.* Grief snatched at Maeve's chest as she drew closer to her destination. She let her mind wander among the scenery.

She imagined a masked stranger lurking among the corn, waiting to strike at unsuspecting victims. This would be the perfect sight for a slasher film, or maybe a sequel to *Aliens* or *Children of the Corn. There I go again, letting my imagination run away with me.* She smiled and shook her head. *Mom always loved my creativity.* Sunrise helped displace the images, even if the general sense of unease tinged with sadness stayed within her.

What am I doing? Launching myself like a missile toward where Mom died? This is probably stupid. No, this IS stupid. The swaying corn gave way to flat rows of cookie-cutter homes, housing additions rolling one after another like a film stuck on repeat. *Indiana sure is boring.* That thought continued uninterrupted as she reached Shady Grove, IN: population 19,325 according to the welcome sign with the chipped orange and white paint.

The bus screeched to a halt, shocking an exhausted Maeve out of her reverie as it jolted her slim frame. She grabbed her duffel bag and shuffled off the bus into the blinding afternoon sunshine. The September air was crisp and cool, a balm to the skin against the sun's searing rays. Maeve shouldered her bag and headed off in the direction of the Airbnb she rented from a local couple, the Grahams. The ad stated that Mr. Graham worked outside of the home, but Mrs. Graham was a former stay-at-home mom struggling with being an empty nester. They advertised a room for rent after their daughter moved out, with meals included at no extra cost. She had been glad for once that her mother had given her the last name belonging to her father, so that the Grahams didn't suspect who she was. On paper, Maeve Baudelaire had no connection to Shady Grove other than a desire to visit.

Maeve was grateful it was not a long walk from the bus stop to the Airbnb. She was tired after her long, sleepless journey. The route into town was obviously meant to be scenic. However, the community had clearly seen better days. De-flowered bushes lined the cracked sidewalk, along with scraggly trees dispersed in equidistant intervals. While the buildings were mostly well kept, several showed signs of disuse and disrepair. There was also a disproportionate amount of bars and hair salons for the supposed population size. The whole walk, Maeve couldn't shake the feeling of being watched. She kept looking over her shoulder, but saw no one who seemed to take notice of her. *I guess just knowing what happened to Mom has me on high alert.*

Maeve came to a halt a mere five minutes from the bus station as she took in the sight of the Grahams' home. The picturesque house was a simple yet elegant two-story made of earthy red brick and featured a wrap-around porch complete with rocking chairs and a porch swing. As an added bonus, the house was only three doors down from the Dickensons and two miles from the copse of beech trees that seemingly swallowed Celia last year. She would have plenty of time to explore and seek closure for the gaping wound in her heart once filled by her mother if she could shake the encroaching disquiet threatening to swallow her whole.

Maeve gathered her courage and knocked on the burgundy door, waiting patiently as she heard the subtle shuffling of feet. A short, stout woman of about fifty opened the door. Her soft brown hair was curled tightly to her head, framing a round, welcoming face. "Hello lovie, you must be darlin' Maeve! Come on in now, ya hear!" Maeve was shocked. She was certainly not expecting southern hospitality in Shady Grove. They were too far north! "Right this way sweet'art. I hope ya don' mind but I made up a pitcha a sweet tea. Cookies are in the oven an' should be done shortly. Your room is upstairs to the right. The bathroom is across the hall. When you're settled, I figured we could get to know one another while we share a glass." The smell of freshly baked cookies tickled Maeve's nostrils, causing her stomach to grumble. It had been too long since she had been mothered.

Maeve's eyes watered at the unexpected kindness. "That would be wonderful, Mrs. Graham. Just let me drop my things upstairs and freshen up." She headed up the wooden stairs, stopping at the upper landing to admire the home. The pastel yellow paint mixed with the streaming sunlight basked the interior in a warm, inviting glow. Framed photographs of Mr. and Mrs. Graham with their daughter dotted the wall, painting a depiction of the ideal midwestern family. There were pictures of fishing, carnivals, marching band performances, and school dances. They looked so happy it was no wonder the woman missed her daughter so fiercely. They had obviously been close. The daughter was a taller, leaner copy of her mom, right down to the sparkling eyes and charming smile. Maeve knew she was going to like it here.

The top of the landing led to several doors, one marked with a paper sign declaring her name. She opened the door and observed the bedroom within. It was painted a misty seafoam color that invoked serenity and tranquility. It also housed a white four-poster bed covered with a quilted bedspread, an end table with a reading light, an armoire, and an antique writing desk. She dropped her bag, quickly sorting her few possessions. Her clothes went into the armoire, her phone and tablet chargers on the end table, and most importantly, her tablet loaded with horror books went into the bedside drawer. She almost brought along some physical copies but wasn't sure how receptive her hosts would be to titles such as *Bunker Dogs* by Gage Greenwood, *Cadaverous* by Jay Bower, and *Lovely, Dark & Deep* by Megan Stockton. She knew some people could get uptight about horror, so she opted to not take the risk since she needed the place to stay. Maeve didn't have many worldly possessions and intentionally traveled light. Other than her pendant, her books were her most prized possessions. She dashed to the bathroom, using the facilities as well as running a brush through her hair and giving her teeth a solid once over. Her business attended to, she skipped downstairs to get better acquainted with her hostess.

Mrs. Graham ushered Maeve over to the soft chenille sofa next to a coffee table laden with the promised sweet

tea and a heaping pile of homemade chocolate chip cookies. Maeve couldn't help but let out a sigh of comfort as
she sat. "Why you're jus' as sweet as cherry pie, dear! So,
what brings a young girl such as yourself to little ol' Shady
Grove?" queried Mrs. Graham.

Maeve chose her words carefully, not wanting to give
away the true reason for her visit. "Well, my mother died
last year, rather suddenly, actually." Maeve paused, the
raw grief catching in her throat. "She was here shortly before she died. After... the incident, I felt so lost. I thought
coming here might make me feel closer to her. Maybe give
me a sense of closure or something."

Mrs. Graham reached forward and gently grasped
Maeve's trembling hand. She attempted to comfort the
fragile girl. "Now, now sweet'art, no need ta fret. You've
got gumption comin' all this way just to be near your
mother. Why, I've been a mom for thirty years and I know
jus' how sacred the mother-daughter bond is. Let's get
a cookie in ya. There's no problem not made betta by
at least a smidgen of warm chocolate." She proffered a
cookie from the tray and Maeve took a tentative bite. The
flavors of decadent chocolate, warm vanilla, and a sprin-
kling of cinnamon swirled pleasantly in her mouth. As

she chewed, Maeve decided she agreed with Mrs. Graham. She now firmly believed that anything in life could be tackled with a little bit of chocolate. "You've had a long journey. Why don't you go take a lie down? I won't wake you, so if you miss dinner, I'll put a plate for you in the fridge. Dinner tonight is chicken and dumplings, from scratch a'course."

Maeve's mouth watered in anticipation. How long had it been since she'd eaten a homecooked meal, let alone something that wasn't ramen or some other ready-made product? But Mrs. Graham was right. She had been unable to sleep on the bus, afraid of the skeevy old geezer across the aisle who kept undressing her with his eyes every chance he got. Creep. "Thank you for your kindness, Mrs. Graham. You're right, I am exhausted." She let out an involuntary yawn. "I think I will turn in for a bit." With that, she grabbed a spare cookie and her glass of sweet tea and headed back to her bedroom. Nestled under the cozy quilt, she began to drift. Just as she fell into the void of sleep, her subconscious swore it heard her mother's voice whispering to her, *Be careful, Maeve.*

Maeve tossed and turned, sucked into a hellish dreamscape. The smell of brimstone assaulted her senses as she attempted to take in her surroundings. *Where am I? A forest?* The trees looked oddly familiar, sinister even, as if they were waiting in anticipation for something. A rustling disturbed the night, followed by a deafening roar. Maeve felt her feet begin to run from the unknown adversary. Her long brown hair streamed behind her as she sprinted in a blind mad dash, not caring where she was going as long as it led to safety. She couldn't outrun the feeling of being hunted by something otherworldly.

Branches smacked her in the face when she wasn't quick enough to dodge them. A sharp one landed a glancing blow to her forehead. Blood streamed from the small cut, but she kept moving, not willing to slow her pace for anything. She didn't know what was chasing her, but she could hear it crashing through the trees after her, making no effort to hide that it was rapidly approaching. It was right at her heels. She could feel its hot breath on her neck. She tripped, her hands and knees stinging with the force of the impact of the hard, rocky earth. A firm grip hauled her to her feet and spun her around. Dark shadows shrouded her assailant. From the corner of her eye, she saw the tail of a scorpion aiming toward her heart. Just before she could take in the face of her pursuer, she heard her mother. "Wake up Maeve, NOW!"

Maeve awoke with a start, her terrified heart attempting to hammer its way out of her chest. The room was beyond frigid, her breath showing as little smokey puffs as she tried to settle herself. Shivering, she looked around for the source of the freezing cold. Yes, the temperature dipped at night in the Midwest, but not like this. Her eyes focused on the window, its lace curtains billowing in the breeze. "I'm sure that was closed before," she thought to herself. She moved to shut the window, securing the pane and locking the mechanism into place. "Even on the second floor, one can't be too careful," she mumbled. She went to shuffle back to bed when she caught her reflection in the glass.

She was still in her pajamas, an oversized Books of Horror t-shirt and cotton shorts. But something wasn't right. There was a small cut, still trickling warm blood, on her forehead. "Hmmmm... maybe I scratched myself in my sleep," she rationalized, until she saw an array of scratches on her hands. "What the hell!" A fresh wave of fear coursed through her veins, causing her to stumble back toward the bed. She curled into a ball, closing her eyes and rocking back and forth. She began to hum a lullaby her mother taught her as a small child, a song intended to ward off evil spirits and demons. She did this for what felt like hours, until she felt the pendant nestled against her breast grow warm. Being the daughter of a medium, she could not overlook the signs. Her mother was trying to communicate with her, maybe even protect her, from beyond the grave. Not for the first time, she kicked herself for not inheriting any of her mother's abilities. They would certainly be useful right now. Something was dangerously wrong in Shady Grove.

Maeve forced herself to sit up and realized the temperature in the room had returned to normal. She crept down the hallway to the bathroom, careful not to awaken the Grahams. In the stark bright light of the bathroom, she took inventory of her injuries. Sure enough, she saw a small, jagged gash on her forehead, in the exact place she had been injured in her dream. Her knees were skinned, and her palms were scratched, seemingly in line with her harsh fall to the ground. Her skin broke out in goosebumps. Dreams weren't supposed to be able to hurt you. She took a washcloth and soaked it in warm water and set about tending to her wounds. After cleaning and dousing them in an ungodly amount of antiseptic cream, she quietly scurried downstairs.

The fear ran its course, leaving in its wake a ravenous young woman. As it was after midnight, and since she'd slept through dinner, she hadn't eaten more than a cookie in twelve hours, and much longer than that since she'd had a solid meal. She devoured the plate of homemade chicken and dumplings, glad no one was awake to see her lick the bowl clean. Somehow, the food was even better than she anticipated. Mrs. Graham was a fantastic cook. Heartened by the meal, she tiptoed back to her room. She went to double-check the window, wanting to be extra sure it wouldn't come back open and freeze her. Seeing the window was secured, she was overcome with tiredness as her adrenaline crashed. Curling back into bed for the night, she didn't even notice the droplets of black ooze splattered on the windowsill. As she drifted off to sleep, a horned shadowy figure hovered at the window, keeping close watch over the Grove's latest resident.

33

Chapter Two: A Trip to the Library

Maeve awoke to one of her favorite smells; cinnamon and buttery vanilla swirled through the air, promising to delight her with heaps of sticky ooey-gooey goodness. The ordeal from last night was temporarily forgotten until she stood. Her skinned knees throbbed as the newly formed scabs cracked. *Owwww, that hurts.* She changed into something more presentable, namely black leggings and a shirt that read "BOOKNERD" across the chest. She rushed down the stairs, leaving her apprehension behind, as she entered the kitchen. Mrs. Graham stood in front of the oven, pulling out the promised cinnamon rolls. "Morning love, I see you got your dinner last night. Why don't we chat a little more while these rolls cool?"

Astounded at the woman's continued generosity, Maeve sat down at the oval wooden dining table. "So, what are your plans for the day dear? Anything I can help you with? My husband, Ronald, has already gone to' work for the day. Ohhhh how I've missed having someone else around to chat with. Goodness gracious Maeve, what happened to your head?"

Sheepish, Maeve brought her hand to the cut on her forehead. "It's nothing, really; I think I scratched myself in my sleep." Mrs. Graham eyed her appraisingly, not quite buying the story, but not prying either. Maeve was caught off guard. In other circumstances, she may have been put off by the older woman. She probably would even have called her nosey. However, Maeve recognized in her a kindred spirit, someone marked by a deep, soul-crushing loneliness. Mrs. Graham needed someone to take care of, and Maeve needed someone to fill the void left behind by her dead mother. She decided to speak candidly.

"I honestly don't know what happened. I just woke up with it. I did have a nightmare, so I probably hurt myself flailing around. I hope you don't mind that I used some of your antiseptic cream." She paused, noticing a look of concern from the older woman. She decided to be cautious and conceal her injured palms.

"I'm fine, honest. Anyway, Mrs. Graham, I was thinking of going to the library to look up some things about the history of the town. Maybe even take a walk down Main Street and see what I can find. I've heard good things about Mr. Ripple's Ice Cream Shoppe. And I always love a good bookstore if you have any recommendations."

Mrs. Graham nodded knowingly, standing to scoop a heaping cinnamon roll dripping in a sumptuous vanilla icing square on Maeve's plate. "Well dear, if memory serves, Shady Grove as we know it, has been around for about a hundred and twenty years. Back before that, it was a French settlement dating to the days of the French and Indian War. The library should have plenty a' local history for you to browse. I highly recommend Mr. Ripple's. Get the triple fudge sundae; you won't regret it. As for a bookstore, I'd recommend Trina's Trinkets and Tomes. That's the local bookstore, and it also sells a wonderful variety of crystals, incense, and the like if you're into that kind of thing. The owner's a real sweetheart, too." Maeve nodded along, trying not to make a scene as she had an internal meltdown over the luscious cinnamon roll. They talked some more, Maeve promising to be home for a nice sit-down dinner to meet Mr. Graham. Finally, with the delicious cinnamon roll finished, warming her heart and belly, Maeve headed upstairs.

She grabbed her small crossbody bag from within the duffle bag, sliding in her tablet, her wallet, and her cell phone before heading for the door. Something in her gut told her to check the window again. Peering toward the pane of glass, she noticed something her sleep-addled brain had missed. Splattered along the windowsill were thick black droplets, almost like fingerprints. Careful not to touch the splotches, she shimmied open the window and looked down. On the side of the house, barely discernible against the brick, were the remnants of a black, claw-tipped handprint. Maeve recoiled in horror, slamming the window shut and fastening it tight. Something had indeed tried to come for her last night. Humming her lullaby, she focused her breathing to calm herself. She decided to add Trina's Trinkets and Tomes to her list of destinations, if not for books, then certainly for a smudge kit. She steeled herself before exiting the room and heading down the stairs. She was determined to not let a strange nightmare deter her from enjoying the local library. Minerva had instilled in her from a young age that libraries were magical, a special gateway to untold worlds and fountains of knowledge. *I could use a little pixie dust right now*, she thought as she exited the home.

Hearing the sound of the closing door, Mrs. Graham glanced toward the kitchen ceiling. She noticed a single drop of black ichor forming, watching it drop onto her clean table. Wiping away the mess, she whispered, "Be careful, Maeve. Not everything in Shady Grove is what it appears."

The library was easily the most gorgeous building in the town. Seated across from the town hall, the distinguished building was three stories of stately brick surrounded by ivy-covered trellises. To Maeve, it looked like heaven. The sign proclaimed— Alain D'Arcy Public Library. *Who is Alain D'Arcy?* She hurried inside, hoping the librarian would be helpful without asking too many questions. "Welcome to Shady Grove Library," chimed a friendly woman. Her name tag read KATIE. "You're a new face around here. How can I help you?"

"Uh yes…" Maeve froze. She hadn't contemplated how to ask for what she wanted without raising suspicions. "Ummm… I have a research project for college, and I need to know about the history of Shady Grove."

"Oh, how fun! That's an interesting project! Are you looking for more foundational history or more recent stuff?"

Maeve grimaced, deciding to chance it with the friendly librarian. "Ummm, the scope of the project is rather large so maybe, uh, both?" Her answer hung in the air between the women, Maeve on pins and needles, waiting to see if the other woman suspected something was amiss. Katie must have really enjoyed her job because, with a smile on her face, she escorted Maeve to a computer with a large side table next to it.

"I'll get you a visitor pass for the computer, and if you wait here, I'll bring you some local history books. All the old stuff is physical media, but a lot of the newer stuff you can find online." Maeve settled in and pulled out the notebook and pencil she always kept in her bag. *Library fairy*. She smiled as she remembered Minerva's special name for librarians. A smiling Katie dropped off two books dedicated to local history, as well as the promised visitor pass, and a bottle of water. "Good luck girl, you got this. I'll be at the front desk 'til 3:00 if you need anything." Maeve thanked her, and then dove in.

She couldn't shake the feeling of being watched. It was just like when she got off the bus yesterday. Something had honed in on her, and the hairs on her neck stood on end. *Stop it! You're just being paranoid*, she told herself. As she reached for the two books, she stealthily took a look around, expecting to find another creep like the one on the Greyhound. However, the library was deserted, other than Maeve and Katie. She grabbed the larger volume, simply titled *Shady Grove: A History*, which appeared to be a promising start. The information was fairly straightforward. Originally a French settlement founded during the French and Indian War by a family named D'Arcy. The town had been officially founded in 1896, as a suburb of Indianapolis. It had been named after the large grove of shady beech trees that had originally populated the area. The grove had been immensely trimmed back, with most of the local buildings utilizing some of the wood. The current forest, measuring roughly five square miles, was all that remained of the once massive span of beeches. The town had grown up around Main

Street, as was evident by the design. Maeve tried to pay attention, but other than the name D'Arcy, nothing was sticking out to her. *I guess it makes sense why his name is on the building now.* She copied the essentials before moving on to the computer.

Upon her internet search of Shady Grove, the first thing she found was a link to an article about the disappearance of Celia Dickenson. Against her better judgment, she clicked on it. She was soon consumed with the story. A beautiful woman in the prime of her life vanished without a trace, just two miles from where she was staying. Staring at Celia's face, Maeve felt a pang of sadness. She clicked off the article, only to find a more recent one. Tomorrow, on the anniversary of Celia's disappearance, town hall planned to host a candlelight vigil in honor of the young woman. Maeve jotted the information down. Maybe she could glean something from the vigil. Probably not, but maybe. Either way, it didn't hurt to honor the missing woman, and by extension, her mother. They both deserved to be remembered after all. She hovered over an article about her mom, a tear already sliding down her cheek. She clicked the link.

She sucked in a breath as a photo of her mother filled the page. Minerva had always been beautiful, but seeing her now made Maeve's heart ache with such intense longing, she thought it might shatter. The poor librarian would have to come pick the pieces of her up from the floor before dropping her into the wastebasket. *Oh, Mom, I miss you so much.* Another tear escaped Maeve's eye. Embarrassed to be crying in public, she went to wipe it away. Her finger came away smudged black.

"What..." Maeve grabbed her purse and sprinted to the bathroom. Her makeup-free face had a black smudge issuing forth from her tear duct. What was going on? She inspected herself in the mirror. *Pale... under-eye bags... but nothing to explain that black smudge.* Maeve couldn't recall the last time she wore make-up. *Maybe a pen leaked or something? Who knows?* She stood gazing in the mirror, worried and confused. She washed her hands, then wet a paper towel and used the damp edge to clear the suspicious smear from her face.

Without warning, the light bulb in the bathroom shattered, plunging the room into inky blackness. "*Run, Maeve,*" a voice whispered from behind her. "Mom?" "*RUN, MAEVE!*" The voice repeated urgently. The temperature in the bathroom plummeted, and Maeve made a mad dash for the doorway. She could see the light from the library hallway through the crack at the bottom of the door. The light abruptly cut off as something moved in front of it. Her internal alarms rang out as she realized she was trapped.

Maeve came to a screeching halt. "Oh no."

A menacing voice taunted her. "Consider this your warning, girl." Maeve's breath caught in her throat. *What was that?* " Your mother made a mistake coming here. I sacrificed her as a warning to the rest of this pathetic town to not mess with affairs beyond their limited understanding. I will have what is due me, and no one can stop me." A slap of air was her only warning before the assault began.

Invisible hands pushed her to the ground and pulled at her hair. She yelped as clawed fingers tore a clump of hair from her scalp. Sharp talons scored her arms and legs, rending fabric and drawing blood with each swipe. *How do I fight an enemy I can't even see?* Malevolent laughter echoed off the empty stalls. "This is just a sampling of what your mother felt before I took my final taste of her. Oh, how sweet her lifeblood was, dripping from her exposed throat as I ripped it to pieces. Will you be just as sweet, child?"

Maeve fought against the invisible attackers, struggling to stand. She slapped at hands she couldn't see, kicking and punching into the darkness. "Ah, a courageous whelp. I will have to break that..." The voice dissolved into maniacal laughter before fading away. The attack ceased as quickly as it had started. Maeve watched as the light from the hallway returned; whatever presence blocked her exit vanished into thin air. Rushing out of the bathroom, she didn't even stop to check her disheveled appearance or assess her injuries. She couldn't help but notice a clawed handprint, like the one from her bedroom window, burned into the bathroom door.

Chapter Three: The Book

Maeve blinked as the shock washed over her, leaving her speechless after her terrifying encounter. Her head swirled in an adrenaline-fueled haze as she walked back to the computer. She haphazardly swiped her belongings into her purse. She didn't care if she looked crazy. She had just been attacked, and she needed to get away fast! She ducked her head, desperate to avoid the librarian, then burst out the front doors. She hid behind one of the ivy-covered trellises as she gulped in large gasps of air in an attempt to fend off an oncoming panic attack. Slowly, her breathing returned to normal and her shaking stopped. She pulled a small compact from her bag, only to gasp at her face.

Blood trailed from the missing chunk of hair, about a two-inch patch right by her part... *I hope that doesn't scar.* Using some tissues, she dabbed at the wound. She covered the patch by adjusting her part, layering hair over the raw skin to hide the damage. Finally, she covered her hair with a black beanie. The last thing she needed as a newbie in town was people thinking she was some sort of hoodlum. She needed to lay low. She would have to return to the Grahams to replace her clothes and cover her injuries. Her leggings were shredded, and not in a fashionable way. They lay in tatters, an assortment of cuts and welts evident underneath the fabric. Her arms fared no better, with a multitude of small wounds weeping for attention.

She sprinted the whole way to the Grahams. Fear held her heart in a vice grip. The house sat eerily silent as she dashed upstairs. *Hmmm... I guess I never took the time to learn what the Grahams do. I just assumed Mrs. Graham was a housewife and would be home all the time.* She gently chided herself as she grabbed a pair of skinny jeans and a jacket to hide the worst of her injuries from eyesight. But first, back to the bathroom for yet more antiseptic cream. She was the unfortunate target of something not of this world; the last thing she needed was to add an infection to her troubles. Maeve shuffled back to her room, enjoying the solitude as she sat on her bed. Loneliness was a constant in her life after her mom's passing. Her breath shuddered as her emotions threatened to overwhelm her. *Mom, I wish you were here. I'm so scared. What the heck was that?* Of course, Minerva failed to answer her daughter. Gathering her courage, Maeve stood. A strange knocking noise kicked her already frazzled nerves into overdrive.

Thump. Thump. Thump. The sound was almost rhythmic in its timing. Maeve's cheeks reddened at the implication. A scream of "Yes, Ronnie, ohmygod, YES!" left no chance for Maeve to deny what she was hearing. *Oh, my hosts are, uh... occupied. I mean, I did say I would be out of the house.* Quiet as a mouse, Maeve tiptoed out of her room. In the hallway, she could hear more obscene bedroom noises. Grunting. A harsh slap followed by a squeal of delight. All while to the beat of the steady thumping. *Wow, I guess they're really used to having the house alone.* Maeve skittered out, noticing a nice pair of men's dress shoes next to a designer women's handbag. *Michael Kors, wow. Mrs. Graham's got style.* Shutting the door to the home as quietly as possible, Maeve couldn't help but think how lucky she had been to avoid detection. *That would have made dinner tonight soooo awkward.*

It was definitely time for that triple fudge sundae. She abhorred leaving the relative safety of the Grahams, but she could never let them know that she had overheard their activities. At least this way, only she had to feel awkward. She walked down the steps and headed to Main Street. She was a woman on a mission as she sped to Mr. Ripple's Ice Cream Shoppe. Mrs. Graham swore chocolate could fix anything. *Well, Mrs. Graham, after the last twenty-four hours, I'm going to test that theory.*

Entering Mr. Ripple's was like walking into a Candyland-inspired haven. The walls were a soft bubblegum pink, with old-fashioned candies in jars lining the counter. The air smelled of innocence and sweet childhood dreams. Maeve breathed it in. *Yes, this is exactly what I need.* Surely nothing bad could happen to her here. She ordered her triple fudge sundae with rainbow sprinkles and extra cherries and took the rainbow-striped dish from the friendly girl at the counter. *I deserve this,* she thought as she took a corner table. She sat at the small candy cane swirl-patterned table and dug into her purse for her phone. Instead, her fingers grazed the spine of a leather-bound book.

"Oh no," she whispered to herself. In her hasty re-treat, she must have accidentally swiped the second history book from the library. *Might as well read through it. I can put it in the drop box on my way back. No need to go back inside,* she reassured herself. She let out a low moan as she took a bite of the best ice cream she had ever had. The flavors of gooey hot fudge, sweet milk chocolate, rich dark chocolate, and tart cherries swirled on her palette. *This is heaven.* Her hands skimmed the cover of the large volume as she pulled it from its hiding place. It appeared weathered, with a dented black leather cover embossed with a now faded pattern of swirls and symbols. The title, printed in a decadent silver scrawl read, *Incantations of Blood.*

Huh, she thought, *this doesn't seem like a history book.* She didn't even recognize it from the library. The history books had been large and heavy, resembling text-books. This was something else entirely. The longer she sat holding it, the more apprehensive she felt. Something about the book called to her, begging for her to devour its contents. The old, crinkled pages all but whispered her name. *Maeve. Maeve. Open me, Maeve.* She delicately trailed her finger down the uneven sheaves. "Oww!" A sharp edge sliced her finger, drawing a drop of blood. She watched, oddly fascinated, as a single droplet of crimson dotted the page. The book seemed... pleased.

Caution took over as she hastily shoved the volume back into her bag. Something was off with this book. Had someone slipped this into her bag when she was in the restroom? Her skin crawled with continued unease. The mysterious appearance of the macabre book ruined her mood. She hurriedly ate her ice cream, the tranquility broken by a rush of paranoid thoughts. From the bus, Shady Grove had appeared as an idyllic, if not slightly rundown, town, but it was becoming obvious that something insidious was afoot. *I should have known better. Something killed Mom, for crying out loud. What am I even doing here?*

Now on edge, Maeve decided her next stop would be Trina's Trinkets and Tomes. She definitely needed to do a purification ritual on her bedroom, and maybe there would be something she could use as a ward of protection. She'd only been in Shady Grove for twenty-four hours, but she had already been the victim of malevolent forces twice. She had numerous inexplicable wounds, and a pit of anxiety and despair roiled deep in her gut. *If this con-*

tinues, I'll be dead by nightfall. Something had to give — and fast.

She kept her head on a swivel as her feet pounded the pavement. Maeve noticed she was sprinting like a bat out of hell. Wild-eyed and frazzled, she had already drawn wary glances from several people out for walks on this warm fall day. A young mother crossed the street with her stroller to get away from Maeve. She knew that she already looked a mess; she didn't need to give off the perception that she was strung out or something. Forcibly moderating her breath, she slowed to a normal pace. Still, she couldn't shake the feeling of being observed like a specimen in a lab. She swore she saw a dark shadow out of her peripheral vision, but every time she turned her head, there was nothing there. The wind brought an ominous warning to her ears, "We are watching you..."

She paused, eyes darting in every direction. She resisted the urge to break back into a run. The delicate hairs on the back of her neck stood at attention the rest of the way. She breathed an immense sigh of relief when, after following Mrs. Graham's directions, she finally arrived in front of Trina's Trinkets and Tomes.

Chapter Four: Sage, Vervain, & Mugwort

A small bell tinkled as Maeve opened the shop door. The heavy scent of incense enveloped her as she entered. At a glance, she could see a variety of trinkets, such as crystals, tarot cards, hanging dried herbs, and even homemade soaps and lotions. She'd expected a true bookstore, but this was more of a mystic's shop with a smattering of books. What was Mrs. Graham up to, sending her here? Regardless, she was happy to be here. The atmosphere instantly put her at ease as it reminded her of countless hours spent with her mother. While not blessed with the sight, Maeve had still been trained by Minerva in various forms of esoteric pursuits. She knew a thing or two about herbs, tarot, demonology, and most other arcane wares.

Just visible behind the counter was an adorable, short woman. Her curls were barely visible under her turban as she spoke to a noticeably attractive giant of a man. They were obviously close, and their height difference made Maeve break out in a grin. The woman broke off their conversation, throwing her arms wide in welcome. "Welcome to my shop! I am Trina and these," she paused, shaking her hands animatedly at the various shop items, "are my trinkets and tomes. Please let me know if I can help you with anything." The man smiled, his teeth bright against his caramel complexion. When his eyes landed on her, she noticed a strange look pass across his face. She blinked, and in an instant, it was gone. *Did I imagine it?* The events of earlier had Maeve questioning everything.

Maeve hesitated as she approached the counter, equal parts eager and nervous to speak to the seemingly inviting duo. She missed how simple life used to be, back before the spirit world killed her mom. She placed one hand on the counter, steadying herself. "Hi, I'm Maeve. Do you have any smudge kits available for purchase? Also, I'd love some recommendations for protection from spirits, if you have any."

"Protection?" the man asked, his eyebrows raising with the question. His intense gaze fell once again on Maeve.

"Yes, uh, I believe something not of this world may be after me and I would like to be prepared." The man obviously wanted to dig deeper, but was cut off by a pointed look from Trina.

"Michael, the smudge kits are over in that alcove." Trina made a big show of pointing to the farthest corner of the shop, where a corner bookshelf showcased smudge kits, candles, and some potted herbs. "Be sure to get Maeve our sage rolled with vervain petals. And don't forget the soapstone bowl, please." The man nodded, begrudgingly setting off to get the kit. *You'll have to wait on your answers, dude.* "In the meantime, I want to hear what is going on." Maeve hesitated, struggling internally on if she could really trust this woman. *Mrs. Graham sent me here... she reminds me of Mom.* The thoughts rattled in her head like runaway marbles.

"Well, uh, it's kind of a long story."

Trina nodded, encouraging the girl as she led her to a couch near the bookshelves. "Michael, lavender chamomile tea with honey please!" she called to her companion. He shook his head at her before heading to the back of the shop. Their interactions helped ease Maeve's trepidation. They obviously had a playful, easy-going friendship. Maybe they could be trusted.

"Ok, I'm not quite sure where to start. I'm uh, new to town, and I've had some crazy experiences since arriving." Maeve launched into recounting her feeling of being watched and her terrifying dream, followed by waking up with inexplicable injuries that mirrored her wounds from the nightmare. She explained the freezing cold and the open window, the black smudges on the windowsill, and the shock of finding the black claw-tipped handprint outside her window. She had to pause before relaying the library incident. She pulled off her beanie and rolled up her jacket sleeves, showcasing her wounds. Trina listened, taking it all in. Her eyes grew wide at Maeve's injuries, but she remained silent.

Michael arrived with the tea and honey, gently placing it on the coffee table before he joined the conversation. He made a show of situating himself in a nearby wingback chair. His brow furrowed as he took in Maeve's injuries. "You say you were attacked..." he trailed off, leaving the implications hanging heavy in the air. His posture screamed that he was willing to take on whoever had done this to her. *Why is he so invested in me?*

"Yes, but not by a man. Something spiritual. I...I think maybe I angered a ghost or something." Maeve clenched her fists, digging her fingernails into her palms. The sharp pain helped focus her, keeping the tears pricking her eyes from falling. There would be time for tears later; for now, she had to be strong. *For Mom. Whatever hornet's nest I've stirred up, this is all connected to her and Celia.* The pair nodded silently, encouraging her to continue unloading her troubles.

"I, uh, found this in my purse as well. At first, I thought I had accidentally taken it from the library, but I don't think that's the case. It's unsettling... it like, absorbed a drop of my blood earlier."

"Absorbed?" questioned Michael. If his eyebrow raised anymore, it was going to disappear into his hairline.

"Uh, yeah. It gave me a paper cut and the blood just soaked in, then was gone. It almost felt like the book was... I don't know, pleased. What do you make of it?" Maeve asked, handing the black leather book across the couch to the mystical woman. Trina gently traced her fingers over the embossing.

"These almost feel like worn-down symbols from another language," she murmured. "Sit tight, I'm going to go make you an herb sachet to wear around your neck. I'll include the heavy hitters: rosemary, St. John's wort, garlic, and mugwort."

"Mugwort? But that aids with..."

"Astral projection, yes. Or lucid dreaming if you prefer that term. Either way, I believe you had an out-of-body experience last night. We need to protect you on all fronts. While I prepare that, Michael will look at the book."

Michael accepted the book from Trina, his fingers caressing its delicate swirls reverently. He observed it from every angle, his expression showing intrigue and apprehension. "No visible signs of anything dangerous," he murmured before gently opening the pages. "Phew, not booby-trapped." He breathed a sigh of relief.

"You thought the book was booby-trapped?"

"Well, more like cursed. There's some malevolence about this and a strange sense of expectation. I agree with you; I don't think this is an ordinary book at all. But I also trust Trina not to just hand me a cursed object with no defenses, so I went with it." Maeve blinked. This man was courageous, and he had such blind faith in his friend that he was either a solid judge of character, or an idiot. "Ok so now that we've established it's not cursed, I would like to ask again. Where did you get this?"

"I don't know..."

"You. Don't. Know?" He said, emphasizing each word. Maeve shook her head. He clearly knew she was holding something back, but he didn't push any further. She couldn't shake the strange look he had given her earlier. He was hiding something, too. She knew now she hadn't imagined it. Still, she detected no malice. If anything, he seemed oddly protective. For whatever reason, he really wanted to help her.

Steel entered her voice, a challenge to Michael. "After I had my encounter at the library, I grabbed my stuff and left. I almost had a panic attack. Later, I found it in my bag. I've never seen it before and the more I look at it, the more sure I am that it's not a library book." She stared right into his eyes, her hazel meeting his brown. *I'm telling the truth.*

Michael nodded, smiling at the obstinate young woman in front of him. "You remind me of someone..." he murmured as he tentatively opened the book. He took great care with the ancient pages. His eyes grew wide as he skimmed the contents. His jaw tightened with obvious agitation as he began to flip through faster. Unsettled, Maeve angled to peer over his arm. She could see cramped, cursive script with hand-drawn images depicting fiendish spells and rituals.

"No, no, it's definitely not a library book. I don't know how this ended up in your bag, but this is a grimoire, specifically for blood magic. An ancient form of powerful, dangerous magic." Maeve recoiled in shock. Blood magic was dark and treacherous. It could be used to summon demons, open portals between the planes, and, of course, to kill. "Based on the quality of the leather and obvious age of the pages, as well as the fading of the ink, I'd estimate this book to date back to at least when Shady Grove was just a settlement, if not further. I-" SLAM! Michael dropped the book with a ferocious crash as the hefty tome fell to the floor, spreading its archaic words to the world. Michael recoiled from the book, clutching his left hand to his chest in shock.

Maeve screamed as blood spurted from Michael's wound. The crimson substance coated the open pages of the book. To Maeve's horror, the tome absorbed the blood, a horrible ritual complete. *Good thing I didn't open that.* The book visibly shook with anticipation at each drop spilled upon its ancient parchment. Michael sprinted toward the back of the shop, away from the blood-thirsty book. Maeve's eyes widened as she saw a bloody finger peeking out from between its pages. Michael's finger. *Oh my God! The book ripped his finger off!* Before Maeve's eyes, the pages consumed the severed appendage, dissolving the flesh and bone into the grimoire. Maeve swallowed the bile rising in her throat. Soon, the finger and all the accompanying blood were gone, absorbed as some sort of hellish sacrifice. Seemingly satisfied, the book shut of its own accord.

"Blo–ood magic indeed," Michael gasped as he returned. A clean rag covered the bloody stump where his middle finger used to be. "Man, now I can't flip a double bird anymore." Maeve chuckled and the tension was broken. It was only then that she realized the man had never screamed.

Trina rushed out with the sachet, "I heard a scream, and I-"

"Trina, that book you gave me contained exactly what it said, incantations for blood magic. AND IT BIT MY FINGER OFF!"

"It did what?" Trina asked incredulously. Michael waved the bloody rag around, vigorously gesturing between the book and his missing finger. Trina blanched at the sight. "I'll be right back with a healing tea of echinacea, calendula, and chamomile. And some dressings for that wound!" She tossed Maeve her protective sachet before hurrying from the room.

Maeve couldn't believe these two. Michael had just had his finger severed by a semi-sentient book about blood magic and the shop owner was off to make tea. "Does it hurt?" Maeve asked, feeling stupid as soon as the words left her mouth. Her cheeks flushed red with embarrassment. *Brilliant question, Maeve. Of course, it hurts, he lost his finger!*

"Like a bitch," Michael said, chuckling good-naturedly as a smile played across his lips. He bent down to tentatively grasp the book by its spine. "I don't want to know what this thing is going to do with my blood. How about you come back tomorrow? Trina and I will have had time to safely investigate this, and hopefully, no one else has to lose any body parts. I hate to say it, but I think you have a powerful enemy." Unable to argue with the man's logic, she left the shop, more confused than she had been when she entered. She started off toward the Grahams when the sense of being watched yet again prickled a warning at the base of her neck.

She turned on her heel, noting the ominous presence was seemingly emanating from the forest. Before she could forget, she attached the sachet from Trina to her necklace. As the sachet hit her skin, she could feel the protective aura take effect. A deafening roar echoed in the distance, shaking the trees. Having been scared enough for one day, Maeve walked as quickly as she dared. She no longer cared that she had heard the Grahams' illicit affairs earlier; she just wanted to feel safe again. She knew she could find that motherly security — square in Mrs. Graham's kitchen.

Chapter Five: Find the Truth

"Maeve, dear, can you help set the table?" called Mrs. Graham. Maeve hurried down the stairs, having just finished freshening up from her intense first day in Shady Grove. The last twenty-four hours had been a whirlwind of unprecedented activity. It started with the nightmare and its corresponding injuries, followed by the terrifying attack at the library, and finished with a man getting his finger torn off by a grimoire of blood magic. Maeve was shaken to her core, but she refused to give up. *I came here for answers damn it, I'm not giving up so easily.* She squared her shoulders before greeting Mrs. Graham with a smile. *Fake it til you make it.*

She followed Mrs. Graham's instructions to the cabinets containing the bowls, cloth napkins, and utensils. Mrs. Graham carefully ladled heaping portions of steaming corn chowder into the bowls while Maeve laid out the napkins and silverware. Fresh flowers accented the middle of the dining room table. The meal was complete with more sweet tea and generous portions of jalapeño cornbread, topped with a sweet and spicy homemade jam. Maeve could get used to eating like this.

Just as everything was finished being arranged to perfection, Mr. Graham came through the front door. He was not what Maeve expected at all. A tall man with a muscular build, he clearly took great care with his appearance. Thick blonde hair and a dentist-assisted pure white smile matched his expensive tailored suit. He seemed out of place in the quaint kitchen. He took off his dress shoes and cast a thousand-watt smile at Maeve. His eyes danced with delight as he took in his wife. "Good evening, ladies," he chimed, as he kissed his wife on the cheek. "You must be Maeve. Pleasure to meet you." He extended his hand, clasping Maeve's for a hearty, welcoming handshake. It was clear to Maeve from the smile, the decorum, and the handshake that this man simply had to be a politician of some sort. Everything about him screamed fake. *How did Mrs. Graham end up with him?*

Maeve's manners won over her inner displeasure. "The pleasure is all mine, Mr. Graham. Your wife is one amazing hostess," she said with a fake smile plastered on her face.

"That she is. After our daughter Rachel moved out, why, we just didn't know what to do. Carol here hadn't cooked for just two in years. Rachel used to have friends over all the time. This place was like teenage girl central for years. It's too quiet nowadays." Maeve nodded along, noticing a barely concealed sadness radiating from Mrs. Graham at the mention of her daughter. She hoped wherever the girl was, that she called home often. "There isn't anyone in the world that cooks as good as Carol Graham," Mr. Graham proudly proclaimed, vigorously patting his stomach for emphasis.

The food was delicious. Mr. Graham dominated the conversation, as he told the womenfolk all about his day. A city councilman as well as a college professor, he was a busy man. He made sure Maeve knew she was always welcome to visit him at work, Bulldog College. He was the dean of students for cultural studies, as well as a tenured professor of history. *If he wasn't so...smarmy, maybe I could take him up on learning some town history. But something about him...he's just too slippery.*

Overall, the Grahams were welcoming, inviting people. Maeve could almost close her eyes and slip into a dream that she was their daughter instead of Rachel. She definitely preferred Mrs. Graham, but she also wondered if that was due to her lack of ever living with a male figure. Her mother had been notoriously single, although plenty of potential suitors had tried to woo her. When Maeve asked her about it, she had answered, "No one could ever compare to your father. I know he's not with us, Maeve, but he would have loved you very much." She never elaborated, but Maeve assumed he was dead. Why else would he not be with them? Regardless, Minerva remained tight-lipped about the man.

Mr. Graham's presence overwhelmed the evening. He talked about the local politics scene, the college, and his day. He left no room for questions or interjections of any kind. *It's all about him,* Maeve thought with disgust. It didn't help that a couple of times she swore she caught him looking at her chest. *Stop being so paranoid. Maybe he's just curious about the necklace. You're a guest in his home. It's normal for him to feel comfortable and you to be uneasy.* Still, she couldn't shake the feeling. *I don't trust him...*

After the meal, Maeve helped clear the table and offered to do the dishes but was shooed off by her hostess while Mr. Graham went to the sofa to watch his favorite sitcom. "He's simply old-fashioned like that. He values his gender roles. He's the provider, and I'm the home-maker. I reckon that's not too common anymore, but it works for us," tutted Mrs. Graham when Maeve protest-ed. "And I can't have a guest doing too many chores; it's not your place. Run along now, dearie." Maeve hesitated, uncomfortable with this dynamic, before heading off to her room.

After taking a shower to cleanse herself of the events of the day, Maeve attempted to read, but nothing was holding her attention after the real-life horrors she expe-rienced. Her scalp ached where hair had been torn out by the root. Thankfully, she had successfully hidden it from the Grahams by carefully adjusting her part. She hoped she wouldn't have a permanent bald spot at the front of her hairline. *That would be embarrassing and hard to explain. I can't exactly go around telling everyone ghosts attacked me in a library!*

Frustrated and confused with how the day had gone, she went back over to the window. Upon inspection, she noted both the windowsill and the side of the house were no longer marred by the black substance from this morning. She didn't pause to wonder if Mrs. Graham had cleaned them, or if they had simply disappeared. Satisfied that she had secured the window, Maeve went ahead and climbed into bed. Her battered and bruised body sunk into the mattress as she drifted off to sleep. Her necklace and its protective charm lay forgotten on the bedside table, removed for her shower, and promptly forgotten.

Maeve opened her eyes to swirling darkness. Goosebumps dotted her flesh as the chill air whipped around her. Squinting, she tried to use the thin slivers of moonlight streaming down from in between dark, ominous clouds to make out where she was. She was struck with the realization that she was perched on the small strip of land just on the outskirts of Shady Grove Forest. The wild grass tickled her bare feet and ankles. In the distance, a sea of tortured voices could be heard, keening in unison. "He's coming. He's going to do it again. Our torturer is never satisfied. You have to help us!" Against her better judgment, Maeve began to walk toward the forest. It was almost as if an unseen force was pulling her forward; a string lanced straight through her heart, compelling her toward the sinister tree line. That's when she saw her; a ghostly form illuminated with an ethereal glow, Celia Dickenson stood at the entrance of the forest. Maeve gasped, "Celia?"

The woman did not respond, instead turning toward the trees, beckoning Maeve to follow. There was no doubt it was Celia. Maeve had spent so much time reading about the case that she would know the missing woman anywhere. Bolstering her courage, Maeve stepped into the trees. Now was the time for answers. This is what she had come to town for.

The darkness was all-encompassing. The meager moonlight seemingly could not pierce both the clouds and the canopy of leaves. She couldn't even see her own hand in front of her face. She followed carefully behind Celia's shimmering form, trusting that she would lead her safely to wherever they were going. Wails of torment echoed amongst the trees, chilling her more than the wind could ever dream of. The wailing grew louder, screams of agony mixed with weeping from countless women. What had happened in this place? It took every ounce of courage Maeve had not to bolt. After about twenty minutes of walking through the dense multitude of trees, Celia came to a halt. Maeve struggled to comprehend the scene before her.

Scant beams of moonlight managed to break through the dense foliage, filtering down and illuminating the outline of a bubbling black pool of thick ooze. An assault of malice and corruption washed over Maeve in waves. She took a sharp inhale before gagging on the stench.

Celia motioned toward the bubbling abyss. "This is the lagoon," stated Celia matter-of-factly.

"The lagoon?"

"This is a sacred place, the lagoon," Celia continued, impervious to Maeve's question. "What remains of me lies here now, trapped in hellish torment, along with my countless forgotten sisters. The forcibly offered blood and bones of centuries of women have been fed to this foul being. Our sacrifice powers this town and bolsters its men. We are nothing but sheep to be slaughtered on the altar of their foul desires."

"Celia, what happened to you?"

"I was foolish, Maeve. I walked into a trap and then...I died."

Gooseflesh surged across Maeve's body. "How do you know who I am?"

"The master of the lagoon knows you. He wants you, Maeve. You encountered him earlier, but he held back. You experienced just a taste of his power. If he has his way, you will be trapped here with us for all eternity. You have to stop him! Find the truth and break the cycle before it's too late for the daughters of Shady Grove!"

Maeve felt her pulse begin to race. "Celia, who is he? What do you mean?"

The same laughter Maeve had been accosted by in the library began to resonate throughout the forest. The ghost woman paused, a look of abject fear passing over her face. "He's coming! Find me in the forest. Follow my trail. The safety of the souls of Shady Grove's daughters rests on your shoulders." Celia reached forward and grabbed Maeve's hand, burning it on contact. "Use this to find the truth. Now wake up, Maeve! Wake up!" Before Maeve could respond, Celia planted two ghostly hands square on her chest and pushed Maeve with all her might. A devilish roar ripped through the forest as everything faded to black.

With a shock, Maeve jolted awake. Safely nestled in her bed, her body felt heavy, as if it didn't quite fit her correctly anymore. She could still feel the weight of Celia's push on her chest. *Astral projection,* she thought, mulling over her out-of-body experience and its numerous consequences. She had developed the ability to leave her body and interact with the spiritual plane. Trina was right. This was very dangerous. Not only could she be harmed in the spirit world, but left unprotected, her body was vulnerable to both physical and spiritual forces. She had to get a grip on this new power, and fast. Her heart ached for her mother. While not able to astral project herself, Minerva would have known what to do to keep her daughter safe.

The hideous roar from her dream echoed through the night. Bolting upright in alarm, she noticed the necklace with the sachet lying on her table. "Oh shit, how could I be so careless?" She slipped it around her neck, feeling her spirit finish sinking back into her body as the herbs did their sacred duty. Taking a moment to collect herself, she stared at her aching hand. On the palm, close to the base of her thumb, a small symbol had been burned into her flesh.

It was an ancient arcane pattern, with dots surrounding a swirl. The very center of the swirl was a pool of black. *I don't think antiseptic cream is going to help this time.* Studying the symbol, she recognized it from *Incantations of Blood. This was on the page that devoured Michael's finger...what does it all mean?* Things were getting seriously weird around here. With a groan, she went to the window, which had mercifully remained closed.

No new black splatter decorated the windowsill, much to Maeve's relief. It was short-lived, however, as a face came into view. Out of the swirling darkness, a pair of glowing red eyes pressed against the glass above a trio of bone-white talons. The creature smirked, revealing a massive maw lined with rows of incredibly sharp teeth, as it drove its talons into the glass. The force of the blow rattled the pane, threatening to shatter it. *I can't let it in here!* Maeve pushed against the glass, feeling the protective power of the sachet travel through her. A ward formed, cementing the window against the evil being. Frustrated, it raked its talons across the glass, leaving a trail that stopped square at Meave's chest, right above her rapidly beating heart. The beast let loose an ominous cackle before tearing off into the night. His cries echoed in the inky blackness, a promise of further terrors to come.

Maeve held her hand to her chest. She swore she could still feel the weight of Celia's frightened shove. The girl's forceful blow had saved her. If she had still been in the spirit world, that creature would have devoured her. If what she had seen was to be believed, Celia was dead, her soul trapped in a hidden area deep in the inner recesses of Shady Grove's forest. Not only that, she was not alone. Those wails she had heard had been a horrifying mixture of terror, pain, and sorrow. How many women were trapped within the confines of the black lagoon? Celia had said centuries' worth of women's souls lay trapped. Her thoughts churned endlessly, and Maeve knew she would not be getting back to sleep. She had to research this symbol, and as Celia had begged, find the truth that was rotting within the shadows of Shady Grove. Crawling back into bed, she grabbed her tablet and decided to read.

Chapter Six: Founding Father

Maeve waited until she heard Mr. Graham's heavy footsteps stomp downstairs and out the front door for work before she exited her room. Even though on the surface he had done nothing wrong last night, something about him had raised her hackles. Maybe it was the way he casually mentioned his daughter, even though it visibly upset Mrs. Graham. Or maybe it was the way he came and went, without offering to help his wife with the housework. While he certainly wasn't showing any glaring red flags, something innate was telling her to be on her guard. *He reminds me of a snake, waiting coiled in the grass to strike.* Maeve shuddered, trying to get that mental picture out of her mind. *Ugh, I hate snakes. Why did I have to think about snakes?* Whatever it was, Maeve didn't mind sneaking one more chapter in to avoid him.

Once she heard a car drive away, she knew the coast was clear. She dressed for the day and crept downstairs. The house was quiet. Mrs. Graham must still be asleep. Without her warm presence, the house felt cold and unwelcoming. Maeve tiptoed into the kitchen to grab a quick bowl of cereal. A picture frame lying face down on the floor, shards of glass scattered around it like crystalline droplets of rain, caught Maeve's eye.

She stooped to pick it up; several more shards of glass filtered to the floor. The pane had been destroyed, cracks spreading across it in such frequency that the contents of the frame were completely obscured. She took a few hesitant steps toward the counter before laying the broken frame onto the granite so she could carefully extract the photo. Thankfully, it was undamaged. It appeared to be a senior picture of Rachel, dated May 2011. *But wait. That would make Rachel at least thirty years old. But I know Mrs. Graham said she was twenty and that she moved away for college.* Something didn't add up here. Deciding she needed to add this to her growing list of things to investigate, she slid the photo into her purse.

Soft footsteps padded down the stairs. "Good mornin', Maeve."

"Hello, Mrs. Graham." Maeve swiveled, hurriedly attempting to hide the damaged frame lest her hostess think she was responsible. The kindly lady ushered her into the living room.

"I'm sorry I don't have breakfast made this morning. My arthritis sometimes makes it hard to get up and get going." Maeve felt a fresh pang of sadness for this woman, doing all the housework with such a painful disease. "After last night, I wanted to talk to you about my Rachel." The woman's voice hitched on her daughter's name. *Wow, she really misses her.*

Mrs. Graham pulled out a photo of Rachel sitting on the couch with three teenage girls. "Oh, these were the heydays of this house. Rachel and her crew. She pointed at her daughter, who stood out already with her perfectly creamy skin and eyes like molten chocolate. "This tall girl was Anya; she and Rachel were best friends from the very first day of high school. I lost track of her after graduation, sadly. This blonde is Stephanie, she works for the Shady Grove Police Department now. And this one," she pointed at a raven-haired beauty with startling green eyes, "this is Scheana. She was Rachel's best friend from diapers. She works with my husband at the college now, as an administrative assistant I think. I'm not quite sure. They have all these fancy names for things that could simply be called secretaries. She stopped coming by after Rachel- Oh, how I miss these smiling faces. The house is too quiet nowadays."

"They're all lovely girls, Mrs. Graham." Maeve couldn't shake the feeling that there was some kind of warning here. Especially as Mrs. Graham's words didn't match the timeline. "But, I thought Rachel moved out to go to college? How would her high school friends be old enough to be on the police force and an administrative assistant at the college?"

The older woman seemed taken aback by Maeve's question. "Oh dearie me, I musta misspoke. Rachel is away at college but for her Masters. Yes siree, my daughter is going to be a biochemical engineer. She has a bright future, my Rachel does." Mrs. Graham put the photograph on the table, a deep sigh escaping her lips. "Well, honey, I best be getting to my chores. These floors ain't gonna mop themselves." Feeling dismissed, Maeve patted the older woman on the shoulder and left.

She stood on the front porch, determined to take a moment to breathe in the fresh air. She sat in one of the rocking chairs, taking in the beauty of the sleepy town. How could some place so peaceful be guarding such sinister secrets? As she mulled over her to-do list, she felt oddly sure of herself. Come what may, she was ready to face it. She needed to check in with Trina and Michael, look into Rachel Graham, and, most importantly, see what she could make of the symbol burned into her hand. What could Celia have meant by following her path? And she couldn't forget the candlelight vigil tonight, even though Maeve now knew in her heart of hearts that Celia was dead. She had seen the very proof last night, on the banks of the accursed black lagoon.

Maeve decided to visit Trina's Trinkets and Tomes first. The woman was obviously more than a common bookseller, and Maeve needed her expertise. Hopefully, Michael wasn't too salty about that business with the book deciding it needed a snack of his finger the day before. The bell tinkled in greeting as Maeve entered. To her surprise, Trina and Michael were waiting for her, coffees in hand, with a third for her on the counter.

"Welcome back," Trina said, throwing her arms wide dramatically. "I felt a disturbance in the spirit plane last night. Dark forces are stirring. Did you dream again?"

Michael handed Maeve the third coffee, the nub where his finger used to be carefully bandaged. His smile erased any reservations she had about the pair. These were adults, well-versed in arcana, ready and willing to help her. Her heart warmed knowing that she had them for the journey ahead. She took a sip of her coffee, delighted to find it was her favorite, white chocolate lavender. Heartened by the sweet brew, she recounted her spiritual travels.

"That's incredible!" exclaimed Michael. "Your second known astral projection, and you made contact with a spirit! Show us this symbol, please." Trina was watching her intently as the teenager presented her hand for inspection.

"Michael, this is from that book."

"It is. It's an arcane symbol related to the dark entity Abaddon. You say Celia Dickenson's ghost burned this into your skin and told you to use it to find the truth?"

"Yes." Maeve was silent for a moment, struggling to process that the supernatural entity stalking her was none other than the angel of death himself. She was grateful to her mom for teaching her demonology so she could recognize the grave peril she was in. "Guys, what would a demon of Abaddon's caliber be doing in Shady Grove? I mean, it's just a small town in Indiana."

Michael and Trina sighed, motioning for Maeve to join them in moving to the back of the store. The space was heady with the smell of an abundant variety of dried herbs and flowers. They sat around a worn wooden table before Michael began. "With Trina's help, I was able to further investigate *Incantations of Blood* last night. She made sure to ward it, so it wouldn't bite anyone again." He shook his hand, the bandages a reminder of the danger. "This is more than just a grimoire; it is a history of the area, dating back to the earliest settlers." He paused, making sure Maeve was paying attention. "The first man to settle here was named Alain D'Arcy. *Incantations of Blood* is first and foremost his journal. Without a shadow of a doubt, he is Shady Grove's founding father. I think you should read it. But first, I want to explain what happened yesterday."

"What do you mean?"

"This is a dangerous book, cursed by its creator. In order to properly decipher the dark knowledge within, one must make a blood sacrifice. When I did not offer one willingly, the book decided to take one of its own accord.

I'm glad you didn't open it in the ice cream shop. Who knows what would have happened."

Chills raced down Maeve's spine. This was dark magic indeed. "But why did it attack you and not me?"

"Simple, you awakened it but did not attempt to read it. Instead of reading just the first couple of pages, where the necessary sacrifice is clearly outlined, I pushed forward. My haste cost me greatly. Who knows how long this evil has slumbered? I'm lucky it was just a finger it consumed. My blood has calmed it for now, allowing us access to its forbidden knowledge. Here, take it. There is nothing quite like reading this firsthand."

With trembling hands, Maeve accepted the open *Incantations of Blood*. Its raw power rippled across the pages, but indeed felt less threatening than it had before. "You're sure this thing won't bite me?" Michael and Trina nodded encouragingly. Still unsure, Maeve began to read.

Chapter Seven: Alain D'Arcy

March 14, 1741

At last, I and my fellow travelers have arrived. We split these last few days from the Vincennes settlement farther south. This is all new territory, as of yet unexplored. We have met several Indians, but they have been friendly and let us pass. All that is here is beech trees. We shall soon clear some to construct buildings, and have fertile ground for planting. I have decided to name our settlement Shady Grove, as an offering to the Lord who smiles upon us with his gift of shade.

April 19, 1741

Spring is to be a time of hope and renewal, but all we have is loss. Our settlement has already lost two newborn babes, a smattering of cattle, and the man who was to be our priest. This is grim tidings indeed. Planting goes slowly, as the yokes keep breaking and the animals are restless. Something in the air of the land seems to keep 'em at a constant fright.

June 7, 1741

Death plagues this settlement. My followers now rumble about a curse. A newly constructed home fell yesterday, crushing the entire family inside it. My Lizbet is heartbroken as her dearest confidant, Winifred was one of the lost. I can only pray to our merciful Father for guidance.

June 30, 1741

Another tragic accident. Charles Myers was out logging with his brothers, James and Jeremiah. A rather large tree fell 'afore the men twere ready. James and Jeremiah twere kill't instantly. Charles, God bless his soul, had his lower extremities crushed. The good doctor tried an save 'im, but after forty-eight hours of intolerable agony, he succumbed to his wounds. We were a settlement of 500, but in nary four months' time, we 'ave lost at least one hundred souls and countless livestock. I fear what the frigid winters may do to our dwindling numbers.

September 10, 1741

The harvest goes slow, with more injuries and death. We are now down to 300, and I fear the worst. I daren't say it aloud, but I dost not believe we shall survive the winter. I shall go out into the woods tonight to pray to God. I have fasted three days and nights. May He hear my prayers and come to our aid.

September 22, 1741

I must tell all that has happened. I went out into the woods to pray, bringing only a candle with me so I might not lose my way. The moon was full, but even the moonlight struggled to light my path through the woods. I walked for what felt like hours, until I came upon a clearing. I did not recognize this space. Mayhaps some other settlers have been here before and cleared this, or mayhaps tis a gift from our Lord, I thought. I fell to my knees, prostrating myself in pure supplication before our Lord. But it was not the Lord that answered me.

A deep laughter, the likes of which I had never heard, rang through the clearing. The trees themselves trembled and fear sank into my heart. The smell of fire and brimstone spread from an unknown source. I was sure I had fallen into one of Hell's pits as complete darkness overtook me. My vision so hindered, all I could focus on was a cold, clear voice. It rang out from everywhere and nowhere at once, beckoning me to listen and obey.

"Alain D'Arcy… would be founder of this settlement. You have fallen upon cursed land, MY LAND!" The voice roared at me, angry. "You have trespassed on my sacred hunting grounds. Did you not wonder how you came here unopposed? This land has been mine since the beginning of time. But I see your heart, Alain. I see the desires you fear to express to even those closest to you. What you desire most is not merely peace, but power. You want to rule these people, make them bow to your every whim. We can work together, you and I."

The man I was two weeks ago would be ashamed to say I did not hesitate. I wanted to know more. The voice called out to me again. "Hidden deep within these woods lies a lagoon, black as Satan's heart, guarded by my minor minions. For a millennia, my minions have stolen women from nearby lands and sacrificed them in my name. I have traveled across the globe, gathering worshippers and creating these pools. This is but one of many, albeit I am to make it my most powerful. Their blood grants me power. However, I would be willing to proffer you a deal, mortal."

"You provide the sacrifices, and I will provide what you seek. Power. Wealth. Protection for your puny settlement. Your family line will live on, as long as once a generation a woman of your line is sacrificed. This will ensure your eternal cooperation. Come, let me show you."

He returned my sight as I stood. I could not help but marvel at the being in front of me. I truly believe he was cloaking the true majesty of his form so as to preserve my sanity. As it was, he towered over me, tall enough to block the trees, his wings large enough to blot out the sky if it had been visible. The behemoth was armored in infernal plating. He had the tail of a devilish creature, curved to a vicious point that seemed to drip a black fluid. I tremble to think of being impaled with such an implement. Before he could speak it, I knew his name: Abaddon, the Destroyer. One of the greatest evils the world has ever faced, he traces back at least to the times of Sodom and Gomorrah. At that moment, I traded my soul. I fell on my face in ardent worship as the demon laughed, delighting in my adoration.

He ushered me forward and I followed willingly. Shrouded in his demonic power, we approached the village of Indians. He pointed at a sleeping woman, lying away from the fire on the outskirts of the village. With his protection, it was a simple endeavor to acquire the woman. With her sleeping form in my arms, he spirited us away to the lagoon.

We were back where we had started, but this time, the lagoon was visible to my mortal eyes. The woman came to, screaming in a language I could not understand. I can only imagine she pleaded for her life. Under Abaddon's gaze, I tossed her into the lagoon. The black waters came alive, thick and vicious as they pulled her struggling figure under. Abaddon spoke, telling me there was power in the watching and in the waiting. We kept vigil until she vanished beneath the lagoon's surface.

Abaddon returned me to the outskirts of the settlement, where he bade me to go back. He explained that my next sacrifice must be of my blood.

I grow fearful. In only twelve days' time, the town has begun to truly flourish. The harvest has been miraculously plentiful, the cows provide an abundance of milk, and the chickens of eggs. I truly believe we may survive the winter now. I carry a heavy burden; whom to sacrifice.

December 9, 1741

Abaddon called to me in my dreams. There has been no death, nary even illness, in Shady Grove since the night of our bargain. He grew weary of waiting for me to uphold my end. I had to make my decision, and make it now. It pained me at first, but I dragged my sister-wife, Lizbet, to the lagoon. She has been barren these last few years, so serves no further purpose to me. Abaddon smiled upon me as she pleaded for her life. I stood by stoically as I watched her die. Her death has empowered me. I grow richer with every passing day, a small stream of coins trickling in here and there miraculously. The children wept, but my daughters are old enough to keep house. I am working on making smart matches, as the lineage must continue on. The women of the land shall feed the demon as he sees fit. He wilt call to me when it is time again. I–

The ink smudged. Maeve couldn't bear to continue. This man had sacrificed his own wife, possibly his daughters and granddaughters, to a demon in exchange for power and prestige. It sickened her that the man's name graced the library. He truly was immortalized in Shady Grove, while his countless victims resided with

Celia in the lagoon. She looked toward Michael and Trina, tears streaming down her face.

"Michael, why was this not visible to us yesterday?"

"The book demanded a sacrifice. Thanks to my missing finger, my blood allowed the book to reveal its secrets. There's so much here. Alain details spells and rituals revealed to him by the demon Abaddon. It appears he was pursuing immortality. We can only hope he did not succeed."

"And you think this is what happened to Celia? She was a sacrifice?"

"It would seem so. She even showed you the pit last night."

Maeve just sat there, trying to take in the wealth of information that had just been aimed at her. She had read the newspaper articles quoting the Dickensons so frequently, her mother's words from the seance came to mind. "Your daughter is neither among the living nor the dead. She is stuck in between, her location hidden from me. Dark forces are at play here. Something sinister is interfering with my sight," Maeve mumbled to herself. It all came into crystal-clear focus. Celia had been sacrificed to the lagoon, like countless women before her, and

Abaddon had interfered with her mother. He had killed her mother!

"I knew it," Trina remarked. Maeve looked at her, wondering what exactly this woman had known all along. "You're the daughter of Minerva Penderghast." Maeve thought about denying it, but opted for honesty instead. She nodded solemnly, keeping her eyes downcast.

"I came here to feel closer to her. Instead, she feels so far away. And now I'm in danger from one of hell's most powerful demons, that apparently has been feeding on the souls of the women of this town for centuries." She felt hot tears pricking at her eyes, but she refused to cry. "Trina, do you have the sight?"

"I do, child. What is it you seek?"

"I think it's time we spoke to my mom. I can't do it alone. Will you help me?"

"Of course, Maeve. We will begin preparations im-mediately."

Chapter Eight: The Seance

True to her word, Trina began preparations for the seance right away. She dashed to the front of the store, furiously switching the sign to "closed" and locking the door. "We certainly cannot afford to be disturbed," she mumbled to herself. Michael shuffled through some drawers until he procured a few deep violet-colored beeswax pillar candles, which he handed to Maeve to begin setting up around the room. The two worked together to open the window and sage the room, creating a clean spiritual canvas for their sacred work. They closed the window, placing a smattering of amethyst, tourmaline, obsidian, and labradorite crystals upon the sill to repel evil and absorb negative influences. The same crystals were strategically placed at the base of each unlit candle, in a further effort to safeguard their endeavors.

Trina drew a circle around the table in chalk and salt, to protect from demonic interference and potential attacks. She made sure to draw it wide enough that even standing, they would all have room to move if necessary. She also set to making new sachets for everyone. This time, the focus was purely on warding off evil. The herbal concoction included chamomile, artemisia, rue, St. John's wort, and sage. "We aren't taking any chances, my friends. Make no mistake, Abaddon will attempt to interfere as we pursue the threads of truth across the mortal and spiritual planes." Maeve felt her stomach clench in fear. Taking a deep breath and inhaling the calming scent of the protective herbs, she squared her shoulders and threw her head back. She may be afraid, but she refused to back down. Her desire to avenge Celia, her mother, the wife of Alain D'arcy, and the countless other women sacrificed to the black lagoon of Abaddon had given her an iron will. She would not falter in her pursuit of ridding Shady Grove of its demonic taint.

"Trina, do you believe it was Abaddon that killed my mother?" Maeve suspected as much, but was ready for confirmation.

"I do, child. I have long suspected Minerva ran afoul of a demon that she was wholly unprepared for. I just never knew which entity. But we will not be caught unawares this time. Have courage. Michael and I will help see you through." The sachets finished, the adults affixed theirs to leather cords and slipped them around their necks. Maeve simply slid hers next to her mother's ashes. Between the pendant and two sachets of protective herbs, she felt a powerful sense of peace. Michael produced a few vials of holy water that he declared were "straight from the Vatican" and set to finishing the purification of the room. *I'll have to ask him about that later*, Maeve thought. The shades were drawn as the candles were lit, their gentle wavering flames the only light in the darkness of the shop's backroom. Their preparations complete, Trina locked the door, securing them in their sacred space.

The three sat around the wooden table, feeling as prepared and protected as they could be. Trina gently placed an ancient mahogany Ouija board and ebony planchette on the table. "Child, I am not as experienced a medium as your mother. My methods are also different. As you are aware, Minerva was an expert at channeling, allowing the spirits to speak to and through her. I prefer to keep control of my faculties and communicate via the spirit board."

Maeve nodded, her eyes glinting in the candlelight. The logic made sense. Channeling left the host vulnerable, which is how Abaddon was able to depose her mother so easily. *Oh Mom, if only you had known.* The Ouija board would allow all three of them to communicate but also react in case of danger. And there would surely be danger. All settled in, Trina cracked her knuckles before instructing everyone to clear their minds and settle their breathing. This was sacred work, after all; they must approach the spirit world with equal parts trepidation and reverence.

Trina cleared her throat, garnering the attention of Michael and Maeve. "We gather here to contact the spirit of Minerva Penderghast, blessed be her soul. I will put my hand on the planchette, letting her spirit guide us to clarity." The woman gently rested four fingers on the planchette, her thumb caressing the side of the dark ebony wood. She began to quietly hum, before transitioning to a soft chant in a language Maeve vaguely recognized as Latin. Finally, the seance began in earnest.

"Minerva Penderghast, we call upon your spirit. Guide us to the truth. Answer us, Minerva. Are you with us?" The planchette began to waver, slowly moving itself to the word YES. Trina smiled, momentarily relishing her success. On the other hand, Maeve felt like she had been sucker-punched. She thought she was ready to communicate with her mom, but now she was overwhelmed with long-suffering grief. Tears welled in her eyes as her heart broke anew. Michael looked similarly stricken. *Maybe he's an empath? Why would he care about Mom?*

"Welcome Minerva. We come seeking your aid, to use your knowledge to assist your daughter, Maeve, in protection and rooting out evil. Tell us, when you sought Celia Dickenson, what did you see?" The planchette bucked the woman's hand off before beginning to move freely. C-E-L-I-A "Ok, Celia... what else?" L-A-G-O-O-N. Maeve shuddered; so her mother had also witnessed the terrifying spectacle that was the lagoon.

"Mom, what is the lagoon?" P-O-R-T-A-L-D-E-A-T-H.

"Portal and death, this isn't good guys," Michael whispered as the planchette took off again. C-A-R-E-F-U-L-M-A-E-V-E.

"I will be, mom. I promise." Trina cleared her throat, eager to get back on track before there could be any interference from beyond.

"What happened to you, Minerva?" D-E-M-O-N. The planchette paused, as if for emphasis. U-N-P-R-E-P-A-R-E-D. "Was it Abaddon?" The planchette zipped to YES before it began to shake. H-E-C-O-M-E-S. The planchette flew across the room as an almighty wind burst through the previously secured window. The force of the gale snuffed out all the candles, plunging the room into darkness.

A loud crash came from the front of the store. The sound of glass shattering and the tinkling of the overhead bell signaled someone had forced their way into the shop. Their footsteps, gunshots in the preternatural quiet, approached the backroom. "Be on your guard; our demon may just have human help." The doorknob rattled as the invader attempted to gain entrance.

This time, instead of fear, Maeve only felt a deep-seated rage. Abaddon, the angel of death himself, had ripped her mother from her. Not just when he had killed her, but now when she finally was able to reconnect with her. She hadn't even gotten to tell her she loved her. Fury boiled her blood as she stood, shouting into the darkness. "I will not fear you anymore! My name is Maeve Baudelaire, and I will hunt you down, break your stronghold on this town, and send you back to Hell!"

A hideous laugh filtered in, a sharp contrast to the sliver of light coming through the slit in the window's drapes. In the sparse lighting, Maeve noticed a dark figure attempting to manifest. "Stay in the circle," commanded Michael. The shadowy figure was quickly coalescing. She could make out an armored behemoth, covered in plated armor, with the tail of a scorpion, and wings large enough to blot out the sky. Michael stood, putting himself between the demon and the women, careful to stay within the confines of the chalk outline. Angrily, he began to chant in Latin. *"Princeps gloriosissime caelestis militiae, sancte Michael Archangele, defende nos in proelio adversus principes et potestates, adversus mundi rectores tenebrarum harum, contra spiritalia nequitiae, in caelestibus."* Michael began to shimmer with an ethereal radiance. "Begone demon! I banish thee!" Drawing a vial of holy water from his pocket, he flung the contents at the demonic form.

Abaddon howled with indignation as Michael finished his prayer. *How dare this mortal man attempt to banish me! I am Abaddon the Destroyer!* Yet, his howls turned to agony as the holy water sank into his form. An acrid smoke filled the room as the demon undulated in fury and anguish. Abaddon shouted, *"Hoc non est super!"* Michael gathered the women to his chest, turning his back to the demon as a force like an earthquake shook the room. Maeve clung to him, feeling immense gratitude that this man she had just met was risking his life for her. She had never felt so protected. As the room quieted and stilled, she opened her eyes.

Fresh sunlight filtered through the room, highlighting the wreckage of everything not within the chalk circle. The cabinet was destroyed, herbs spilling out across the floor in heaps. Picture frames lay shattered on the floor. Candles spilled hot wax where they had once stood. The crystals had cracked and split, some even crumbled into dust. Everything was coated in a smattering of thick black droplets. "Demon blood," Michael whispered in awe.

He released the women, but Maeve hugged him again. "Thank you, Michael."

"You're welcome. I always protect my own."

"Sorry about your shop, Trina." Guilt settled into Maeve's heart. Trina had risked everything for her to be able to talk to her mother, only to have her backroom destroyed. They hadn't even seen the front of the shop yet, but she could imagine. And there was still the mysterious intruder to contend with. The doorknob had stopped rattling, but they had not heard any retreating steps.

The older woman simply shook her head. "It is okay. I can rebuild. What matters most is we have our answers. We have also engaged a powerful demon and lived to tell the tale. What is it he said, Michael?"

Grimacing, Michael translated the demon's parting words. "This is not over."

Chapter Nine: Secrets Revealed

Maeve took in Michael's words. Abaddon had issued a warning to the group. He was coming for their town, for them. The realization hit Maeve like a ton of bricks. She had just referred to Shady Grove as her town! She hadn't been here for even forty-eight hours. Yet, in spite of all the sinister happenings, she felt oddly at home here. She could actually picture herself living here. She envisioned hanging out with Trina and Michael, spending countless hours at the library once it was cleared of demonic influence, and eating her weight in triple fudge sundaes. She could even see herself attending the local community college one day. But in order to have a future in Shady Grove, or anywhere for that matter, she had to first vanquish the demon.

Michael put a finger to his lips, using his other hand to gesture at the door. He was right. They had no way of knowing who or what was out there. Trina pulled the drapes open, allowing Michael to find a mangled piece of wood he could use for a weapon. Assuming a defensive stance, he opened the door. Maeve gasped.

The front of the shop was as bad as she had feared. Crystals were scattered everywhere, some pulverized by the force of the blast. Claw marks marred the bookshelves and the glass display cases. But human hands had smashed the crystal ball, as evidenced by the smear of bright red blood among the shards of glass. Books were flung everywhere. Tarot cards littered the floor, all face-up showing Death. It looked like a tornado had gone off in the middle of the shop. Black ichor dripped from the ceiling. Trina looked upward as a thick droplet splattered across her nose.

"Demonic work is brewing. A dark tide rises over Shady Grove, and we are simply adrift in the sea. We must hunt for the resources to vanquish this evil before it is too late." Michael and Maeve nodded solemnly. "What bothers me most is the human aspect. Someone must have carried on Alain's legacy, but who? And someone was here during the seance. Abaddon's minions? Someone else? Are they one and the same? Or do we have more than one person aiding the demons?"

With a sigh, Michael replied, "I can start researching my family tree. The name D'Arcy is no stranger to me...it runs throughout my mother's side."

Maeve and Trina's heads swiveled in unison, their twin stares boring a hole into his chest. "You're related to Shady Grove's founder?" Maeve asked.

Michael shrugged. "It all makes sense. The book wanted to reveal its secrets to me. It seems to believe I am the rightful heir. Trina, we only scratched the surface last night with Alain's confessions. The back of that book is full of dark rituals. We need to investigate. Time is of the essence."

"Yes, yes, of course. Let me straighten up here and gather some materials." With that, Trina hastily pushed Michael and Maeve from the shop. *She probably wants a minute to collect herself. I know I would if a demon pulverized my life. I mean, he killed my mom and I still don't have it together.* Steadying her thoughts, Maeve looked around. She was amazed that from the outside, other than the broken glass on the front door, the building looked no worse for the wear.

Michael turned to look at her. "I think it's best if we stay together for now. You have a demon after you, and I think we need to know why. It has to be more than just your mother."

"You and Trina act like you knew my mother. Other than her brief visit here, I don't see how that's possible. She was from Michigan."

Michael paused, clearly weighing his words. "We did know Minerva, but we hadn't been in touch in years. She saw Trina briefly before... before she died."

"Oh..."

"Yeah. It weighed heavy on Trina's heart that she didn't pick up that there was something more to Celia's case. When Trina broke up that seance and found your mom, well, we were both devastated. I don't think she's ever forgiven herself. She barged in at the end of that doomed seance, but it was too late. She was able to help save Mr. Dickenson, but your mom...she was too far gone. I think it has done wonders for her, meeting you. We didn't even know Minerva had a daughter until you walked into the shop. You're the spitting image of her when she was your age."

Maeve struggled to process everything. Regardless, she had to ask one more thing. "So, Michael, how DID you know my mother?"

The man sighed. "I don't know why she never told you, Maeve. Your mom grew up in Shady Grove. This was her hometown."

Maeve's brain came to a screeching halt, her synapses firing at the speed of light, yet unable to comprehend what she had just heard. "No, no, that can't be. She grew up in Michigan."

"No Maeve. She ran off as soon as she turned eighteen. She left in the dead of night, not saying goodbye to a soul. She must have started over because the next time we heard of her, she was a renowned medium. We both tried to contact her, but it was always radio silence."

"Do you know why she would do that? And why she lied to me about it for all these years?"

Michael opened his mouth to speak, then hesitated and shook his head. "I thought I knew Minerva well, once upon a time. But now I wonder...." He trailed off, seemingly lost in his reverie.

After a brief detour to get some chocolate ice cream in their bellies, the duo went to Michael's house. Another stately brick home, it stood out for its collection of horror garden gnomes dotting the neatly manicured lawn. Maeve waved at Freddy, Jason, Chucky, and more horror legends. Michael ushered her through the front door and into the parlor. A well-loved leather sofa faced a fireplace that Michael immediately began attending to. Maeve was overwhelmed by the sheer number of books lining the walls. Other than the fireplace and the door, every conceivable inch of wall space was taken up by bookshelves.

Michael informed her he was a security officer at the local college, but he was also a dabbler in arcana and an aspiring author. While he was not blessed with the sight like Minerva and Trina, he was well-versed in demonology and exorcisms. Maeve brought up the holy water and Michael laughed. He explained he had a friend that had joined the papacy, and occasionally ferried Michael some holy water, just in case. He was now the owner of a veritable arsenal of the precious liquid, something that may come in handy later. He also explained Latin was the most powerful language that could be used against demons. When he faced off against Abaddon, he had chanted the beginning of the prayer to St. Michael, in its original Latin. *Hmmm...Mr. Graham is a history professor. I wonder if he knows any Latin that could help us. I'll have to ask him later.*

Michael hustled off to make some tea, leaving Maeve to explore his rather eccentric library collection. He had indie horror books next to Stephen King next to books of Latin prayers and the hierarchy of demons. She reached for a leather-bound tome that caught her eye titled *Angelus Abyssi*. Inside were handwritten drawings of Abaddon in his various forms and a list of his various names. *Now THIS will come in handy.*

"Abaddon, also known by the name of Apollyon, is the angel of destruction. He is known by many simply as the destroyer. He is also the angel of the abyss, which pertains to the pit of destruction mentioned in various religious texts. Do not be fooled by the name angel, however. He is a fallen angel, similar to Lucifer the Morningstar, and possesses many similarities to demons.

His main forms are a human male, a human male with wings, and a human male with the head of a locust. He also has what should be feared above all others, his true form. In his true form, Abaddon resembles a large horned behemoth wearing iron plate armor, sporting the tail and deadly stinger of a scorpion, the teeth of a lion, and large wings. No one knows the true origins of Abaddon, but he is known in various texts for his bloodlust, love of torment, and his role in the eventual end times. It is said that his stinger will torment the unprotected. Abaddon and his abyss are usually noted as sharing a name, with his abyss of destruction being a pathway to torment and hell. Those found to be facing Abaddon should be well prepared, as he cannot be killed, but he can be banished from the mortal plane."

Maeve dropped the book, stunned. "Michael!"

"What?"

"I think I found why Abaddon is so interested in Shady Grove. I think when Alain D'Arcy made his deal, it was more than just a sacrifice. He anchored the town to Abaddon, not just the demon but his pit. The abyss into hell. The lagoon was already there, but that deal..it's all connected."

"Oh shit. That puts things into perspective," he replied.

Michael spread her arms wide. "My lineage, I am of the D'Arcy line, as we already discussed. Reading the *Incantations of Blood*, it all makes sense. The women in my family — they don't live long. There's a lot of unexplained death there, while the men are very powerful. But over time, the family has dwindled."

He sat, holding his head in his hands. "That's why I became such good friends with Trina and your mother. Between their rituals, spells, herbs, and potions, they were able to keep me protected. When your mother left, I delved as far as I could into demonology, exorcism, religion... anything I could find. My mother died during childbirth. The doctors said she died chanting incoherently."

"What was she chanting?"

"A prayer of protection for me... until recently, my theory was Abaddon couldn't touch me because she gave her life for mine. Four members of my family died the year I was born. I believed that between my mother's sacrifice, the extra protection of Trina's herbs, and my knowledge of the arcane, he couldn't touch me. Now we know I was never in danger in the first place. The demon only goes after women."

"What about the pit?"

"As there are fewer D'Arcy's around to sacrifice or be sacrificed, I think Abaddon has been taking more people from the town, like Alain did with that native girl, just to feed his bloodlust. Poor innocent souls like Celia Dickenson. He may even have help from someone willing to bargain with a demon."

"Okay, Michael, this is all very enlightening, but what does this have to do with why my mother ran away from home nineteen years ago?"

Michael looked at Maeve sheepishly, a dark blush coating his cheeks, nose, and even down to his neck. "Well, Maeve, I don't know quite how to say this, but uh... I believe she was trying to protect you." He hesitated, obviously weighing the impact of his next words. "Maeve, I think I may be your father."

Chapter Ten: Ties that Bind

Maeve stared at Michael like a deer in headlights, her heart racing as her mind spun off in a million directions at once. "You think you might be WHAT?"

Michael turned to the bookshelf, pulling down a photograph of three teenagers: Michael, Trina, and what was unmistakably a young Minerva. Michael had his arms around both of the girls, but Minerva was planting a kiss on his cheek while Michael was grinning like a fool in love. Sighing, he handed Maeve the photograph. "She was the love of my life, your mother. When she left in the dead of night nineteen years ago, she didn't even tell me goodbye. A lifetime of friendship, three years of dating, gone in a flash. I never stopped looking for her. She finally agreed to meet with me the day after the Dickenson seance. She tracked down Trina and told her that she had something important to tell me. As we both know, she never got the chance."

"You think that important thing was... me? She found out she was pregnant and ran away," Maeve stated matter-of-factly. Part of her couldn't wrap her mind around her mother leaving everything she ever knew behind simply because she was pregnant, but part of her could. Minerva was notoriously proud, and she wouldn't have wanted the small-town shame of being yet another pregnant teenager. And the timeline DID fit.

"I do, but not for the reasons you think. She loved you, Maeve. That much is obvious. My theory as to why she took you away from this town and hid you from me is simple. Remember, for all these years, we've speculated that my family is cursed. We just didn't know how or by what. But by leaving, she was able to protect you. You see, you have D'Arcy blood in your veins...that's why Abaddon locked onto you immediately. That's also probably why he killed your mother. She hid from him what he deemed his due, even though she didn't quite know that's what she was doing. He wants you to be his sacrifice." Michael paused, letting his words sink in. "But not on my watch."

Maeve sucked in her bottom lip, worrying about the implications. "When did you first suspect I might be your daughter?"

"The moment you walked into the shop, the spitting image of your mother, but with my eyes. I couldn't help immediately doing the math. It all adds up. Especially since I was only seventeen. When you're teenagers, that one-year age difference can be nothing and everything all at once. Minerva knew I couldn't leave with her, so she did what she deemed necessary to keep you safe. She may not have known what exactly the curse was, but she figured out enough to at least know you needed protecting. I just wish she had known the whole truth...maybe then her death could have been prevented."

Maeve looked at Michael through a new lens. She had always known she was almost a carbon copy of her mom, but now she could pick up some similarities between her and the man in front of her. It was there in the eyes, the slant of their noses, and endearing, slightly crooked smiles. Michael continued, "Baudelaire was my mother's maiden name; she gave that to you. And Maeve was my grandmother, the woman who raised me. Your mother gave me all the signs."

Maeve opened her heart to the truth standing right before her eyes. Michael beamed, opening his arms to envelop her in a bear hug infused with all the fatherly love she had missed in her young life. The two held onto one another, a tidal wave of bittersweet emotion washing over them. They were happy to be reunited, to be able to know and love one another. Both of them felt the deep ache of Minerva's absence.

"I wish your mother was here to see this, to see us." Tears welled in Maeve's eyes.

"She'd have been so happy we found each other." Locked into a long overdue embrace, the two wept.

"Okay, Maeve, I think you should go have dinner with the Grahams. I hate to let you go now that I've found you, especially now that we know Abaddon has set out to make you his next victim. You're the last D'Arcy daughter of Shady Grove. But we need to keep up some semblance of normalcy for the outside world. We know Abaddon has at least one human helper, and we aren't any closer to finding out who that is. I'll stay close to the house, study the book, and look around to see what I can scrounge up for a fight. I have heaps of holy water, but we're going to need more than that to have a hope of banishing one of the oldest, most dangerous demons out there. Trina and I will meet up with you at the candlelight vigil for Celia Dickenson tonight."

Maeve wiped away her tears before nodding. She was terrified, but it was time to be brave like her mom. "So, do I call you Michael or Dad now?"

Michael cracked a smile that could steal the combined light from the sun, moon, and stars. "I would be honored if you would eventually choose to call me Dad. But that is a choice only you can make, hon. I won't push you one way or another."

"Dad it is," she said, testing the weight of the word on her tongue. It would take some getting used to, but it already felt right. *I'm not alone anymore. I have a dad!* Maeve smiled to herself as she gave Michael a quick parting hug. She knew she had a lot of information to process in a short amount of time. She was the target of one of the most dangerous demons because of an ancient deal made by her dastardly ancestor, Alain D'Arcy, who had most likely tethered a portal into hell in Shady Grove. Oh…and she had a dad. Her head spun as she entered the Graham's, happy she made the journey unaccosted.

Walking in, she was greeted by the mouthwatering smell of pot roast, carrots, onions, and mashed potatoes. Mrs. Graham was a flurry of motion in the kitchen, adding a dash here and there of finishing seasonings to each part of the dish. "Maeve honey, you're home! I mean, back. Oh, I'm sorry, you really can't take the mothering instinct out of a mother."

Despite everything that had transpired over the last forty-eight hours, Maeve couldn't help but laugh. "It's okay, Mrs. Graham, I really don't mind." Her laughter caught in her throat when she noticed something that hadn't been there when Mrs. Graham had come downstairs this morning.

"Mrs. Graham, your eye!" The older woman's left eye was swollen shut, turning ugly shades of purple, yellow, and green. She was obviously embarrassed, and that inflamed Maeve. "Did your husband do this?" Mrs. Graham refused to meet her gaze, shame evident in her stance. "I slipped on the stairs and hit my head." She shook her head in a weak denial as she spoke, but Maeve knew the truth. She felt her blood boil. *Shocker, the politician is also an abuser.* This sweet, kindly woman deserved so much better.

"When did this happen?"

Mrs. Graham slowly shook her head as several tears trailed down her face. "I took something from him, and now he can't get it back. He caught me looking at the picture and... he would prefer I act as if Rachel never existed. She left, and to him, that means she's as good as dead. He brings her up only to spite me, as if he can use a mother's love against me as a weapon. He broke that picture frame this morning. But this...well we shan't speak of it." Maeve had to consciously unclench her fists before hugging her hostess. She felt Mrs. Graham steel herself during the embrace. Even though the situation was obvious, the older woman clearly wasn't ready to admit what exactly was going on. *How long has this been happening? He's gonna pay for this.*

Slowly, Mrs. Graham pulled away, dabbing at her eyes with a handkerchief. She winced at her swollen eye, but steeled herself. She stood up and resumed the final preparations on the roast as if nothing was amiss. They set the table in relative silence, Maeve following Mrs. Graham's lead. When the older woman's back was turned, she spit into Mr. Graham's potatoes, being sure to mix it in before topping the pile with a heaping portion of gravy. *That'll serve that bastard right.* This small act of rebellion fortified Maeve's spirits. She made a solemn vow over those mashed potatoes. He would not get away with this on her watch. He might not be a demon like Abaddon, but Mr. Graham was an abuser, and in her book, those two things really weren't that far apart. The front door opened, and the assailant entered while whistling a cheerful tune. Maeve hated him with every fiber of her being.

She had to work hard to keep a smile on her face as Mr. Graham lowered his face to his wife's for a kiss, only to stop to brush a delicate curl away. "What happened here?" he murmured. Maeve restrained herself when Mrs. Graham winced in pain.

Mrs. Graham murmured a made-up excuse about getting hit with a falling object. *She changed her story...I knew it!* The Grahams' performance of a happy, loving couple made Maeve sick to her stomach. *How do people live like this?* She had to constantly remind herself that her face could not spill the proverbial beans. As much as she wanted to help her hostess, she needed to be smart about it. Picking a fight over dinner in their kitchen was not smart at all. This man was dangerous. *I'll talk to Dad, he'll know what to do. Or maybe Rachel's friend, Stephanie, the police officer.* Somehow, they made it through the meal, both women releasing a sigh of relief when Mr. Graham went upstairs for a shower. Maeve gloated inwardly that Mr. Graham had eaten every single bite of the tainted potatoes.

"Well, I'm glad that's over," Maeve whispered. Mrs. Graham simply nodded. "You have to let me help you."

"You don't understand Maeve. I'm not from here. I'm from Tennessee. When Ronald swept me off my feet, we came back here to his hometown. I've been nothin' but a housewife from the moment we got married. I've never held a job. I have no prospects outside of this life. The thought of poisoning him has crossed my mind a time or two, but I'm just not the type. No matter how much he hurts me, I can't bring myself to fight back. Besides, after... losing Rachel, there's nothing left he can take from me."

"That's not true Mrs. Graham."

"Oh, sweetie. Things may be all cattywampus, but they could be worse. There are many fates that you can be subjected to that are worse than death." The two women embraced as Mrs. Graham dismissed Maeve. The younger woman was heartbroken for her companion, but didn't have much time to dwell on it. The sun was beginning to set, meaning it was time to meet her dad and Trina for the candlelight vigil in Celia's honor.

Maeve easily found her compatriots thanks to her dad towering over the crowd. She could not believe how easily he had slotted into the role in both her mind and heart. Growing up, she had grilled her mother about her father, only to be met with wistful sighs. All she would ever say is she had loved him deeply. She had always insinuated that if it was up to him, he would be there with them. Maeve assumed he was dead and it was just too painful for her mom to talk about. She couldn't imagine losing the love of her life. Minerva had taken his identity with her to the grave, something Maeve had lamented at the time. Now, having met Michael, Maeve could see both how right her mom was and how different her life could have been. He certainly would have been with them if he had been given the chance. Michael had already proven himself to be valiant and courageous, as well as intelligent and selfless. While they may have lost nineteen years together, they had the rest of their lives to reconnect. Maybe he could even help with the situation with the Grahams. Surely some of his books held information on curses.

Maeve slowed as she approached City Hall. Trina sprinted across the crowd and grabbed her into a hug that said more than words ever could. Never before had a hug communicated such love, pride, grief, and fierceness. "Michael told me the news! I suspected, but figured it was best to let the two of you figure things out. I've done enough meddling in my life. Welcome to the family, Maeve!" The woman's eyes danced with merriment. Michael stood there, obviously letting Maeve lead. She gave him the first of what she hoped would be many father-daughter bear hugs. The trio grabbed their candles, centering Maeve in the middle of the group. Maeve's joviality curdled as she saw Mr. Graham accompanying Mr. and Mrs. Dickenson to the front of the crowd. Mrs.

Dickenson could not control her weeping as she clutched an enlarged photo of their daughter.

Mr. Graham tapped the microphone, "Testing 1, 2, 3..." *Ugh, all politicians really are cut from the same old boring cloth.* An electronic screech blasted through the speakers. Mr. Graham looked murderous as the tech crew fumbled to adjust. When silence resumed, he loudly cleared his throat. "We are gathered here today to honor one of the lost daughters of Shady Grove, Celia Dickenson. Celia has been missing for one year, and with your continued support, we know we can bring her home. She's out there...somewhere, waiting for us to find her."

Maeve grimaced as the crowd roared with applause, lapping up every word the blonde man said as if it was manna from heaven. *He really has the town wrapped around his finger.* The crowd grew silent again as Mr. Dickenson took center stage. Sweat beaded on his brow as he struggled to gain his composure. Mr. Dickenson took a deep breath, his voice wavering before growing clear and strong. "Thank you, everyone, for coming out tonight. It has been one year since our daughter, Celia Dickenson, was taken. Yes, folks, you heard me right. Taken. Police have found new information confirming that Celia was lured into the woods last year. I..."

Mr. Dickenson's voice caught in his throat, bloody foam coating his lips as he fell to his knees, clutching his chest. Black ichor poured forth from the wound he had sustained all those months ago at the seance. Screams erupted from the group as the substance became visible to the crowd, soaking the man's shirt at an alarming rate. Mrs. Dickenson ran to her husband, attempting to staunch the flow of ichor. Tears streamed from her eyes as she begged someone, anyone, to call 9-1-1.

A shadowy figure caught the attention of the trio as it darted away from the vigil. "Abaddon strikes again," Michael whispered. Sirens split the air as paramedics arrived, adding to the rising pandemonium. At the edge of the action, unmoving, Maeve caught a young woman staring at Mr. Dickenson. Her short raven-black hair and stylish white pantsuit helped her stand out. She looked oddly familiar to Maeve, but she simply couldn't place her right now. But what really caught her eye was Mr. Graham beside her, his hand resting lower than acceptable on her waist, where the handbag she had seen by the door of the Grahams rested. *Cheating bastard!*

The woman muttered something unintelligible as Mr. Dickenson began to seize. The crowd swarmed and Maeve lost sight of the pair. The paramedics set to their grim task, but to no avail. Mr. Dickenson died in his wife's arms, in front of the crowd assembled to honor his daughter, her name the last word on his lips.

Chapter Eleven: Demonic Interference

Anne Dickenson's wails of despair split the night. She cradled the lifeless body of her beloved husband as she rocked back and forth, screaming to the heavens, "Ed! Please, no! Don't leave me, Ed!" The paramedics gave her space as she burrowed her face into his neck, gut-wrenching sobs shaking her fragile frame. In a year, the poor woman had lost both her daughter and her husband. Her soul-rending lament displayed to the entire town that she would never be the same again.

Michael bowed his head in respect, muttering an ancient blessing for the deceased. Beside him, Trina's brow creased in worry. Maeve fought the urge to hunt down Mr. Graham, but she knew now wasn't the time or place. As the crowd descended into chaos, the shadowy figure, further in the distance this time, caught Maeve's eye again. *What is that?*

Maeve whacked Michael in the chest to get his attention. "Is that...?" Before she could finish her question, Michael broke away from the crowd. Maeve and Trina shared a questioning glance, then followed Michael, sticking to the shadows as the three of them trailed the mysterious figure toward the nearby park.

As Maeve's foot crossed the threshold between pavement and grass, the figure vanished! *That can't be good. Is this a trap?* Maeve kept her head on a swivel as she searched for any clue as to where the mysterious creature had gone. Beside her, Michael assessed the area for threats; his paternal need to protect her surging into overdrive. He paused to take in a wooden bench flanked by two saplings. A flickering street light struggled to stay on over the dimly lit area. *Well, that doesn't seem suspicious at all...*

Michael eyed the bench, his eyebrow arched so high it almost merged with his hairline. "Creepy," he murmured. He approached cautiously before ultimately deeming the area safe. He sat on the bench, then patted a spot beside him, ushering Maeve to his side. He huffed, "So, do we all agree we witnessed Abaddon or one of his minions kill a man?" Both women nodded.

Trina responded, "I believe he just put poor Mr. Dickenson on display. Probably to send a message to us. Those who interfere with Abaddon's work will be swiftly punished. I don't know how much longer my wards will be able to prevent him from having his way. Yes, they're powerful enchantments, but I've never tested them against anything like this! Before we run out of time, I think we need to find his human helpers. We know he has at least one person carrying on Alain D'Arcy's dirty work."

"I actually have an idea of what happened," Maeve interjected. "So, do you remember from the seance, Mr. Dickenson was pierced with an unidentifiable weapon? We already know Abaddon was there that night. From what we saw in our attempt to communicate with mom, the demon appeared in his most powerful form, including his scorpion tail. What if the weapon was the tail, and it just took nine months for the poison to finish him off?"

Trina paused to contemplate Maeve's words. "That would make a lot of sense, actually. I noted poison in the wound that night and did my best to cure it. But that man did not know a day without pain since the attack. Anne's memory might have blurred, but she still regularly made her way to my shop, seeking relief for poor Ed. With demonic poison of that caliber, it could have lingered in the wound, making him suffer until, well..." she motioned toward the commotion.

A sudden hissing sound drew the attention of the trio. *Please, no.* The flickering street light illuminated an inky black shape slithering toward them. A mass of scales at least ten feet long curled upon itself, the snake's fangs glinting just as the street light gave up the ghost. The area plunged into darkness. The last thing they saw was the snake's eyes, glowing with hellfire and hatred.

"Dad..." Michael instinctively moved in front of Maeve and Trina as he pulled a knife from his belt. Maeve shuddered, finding it difficult to be brave in the face of her greatest fear. *Noooo! I hate snakes!*

"Ssssss- Abaddon sssendsss hisss regardssss!" the snake's menacing voice spoke in Maeve's head. From the look of shock on Michael and Trina's faces, she assumed they heard it too. "You mortalsss don't know what you're up againsssst." Trina flicked a lighter on, the dancing flame adding to the demon's malevolent aura. Its eyes flashed with malice as it lunged for Michael's throat. Maeve screamed as Michael raised his arm, slicing down with the wickedly sharp blade. The snake hissed as the knife sliced a deep gash into its underbelly.

Trina thrust the lighter into Maeve's hand. "Hold this." The snake regrouped, ichor falling like spilled ink upon the grass. Trina produced two thick blades, causing Michael to raise an eyebrow. "What? I wanted to be prepared. Can't let you have all the fun!" She laughed as the snake lunged again, this time aiming for Maeve. Michael pulled her to safety as Trina's blades danced through the air.

The snake's head toppled to the ground, demonic blood spurting from its many wounds. Trina had sliced the viper into ribbons. "Thisss issn't over...don't you know demonsss can't be killed! Abaddon hasss legionsss..." The snake's voice faded as its wretched essence retreated back to Hell. Michael groaned.

Maeve turned to her father, noticing a small nick on his wrist. "Dad, you're hurt!"

Trina sucked in a breath. "That's sure to be some unholy poison. Should I..." but Michael was already dousing the wound with holy water. He gritted his teeth as smoke issued forth, the blessed water cleansing the wound.

"Damn, that hurt."

Trina arched an eyebrow. "Noted, snake bite trumps losing a finger somehow."

"Hey! I was in shock then. And this was a damn demon snake. Of course, it hurts!" Maeve chuckled at her dad's retort, breaking the tension. She wrapped her arms around Michael for a hug that both of them desperately needed.

"Thanks, Dad. I really, really, REALLY hate snakes."

"You inherited that from your mother, I see," he smirked.

Trina interjected, "Look, I hate to break up this family moment, but we're not safe here. Michael, we need to get to your house. Surely something in your collection will be able to guide us toward answers." Michael nodded grimly, the mood darkening just as quickly as it had lightened. In the distance, they could still hear the commotion from Celia's vigil, the sound of screaming and crying masking the demonic assault the trio had just endured. *We're lucky to be alive*, thought Maeve.

Fear settled in Maeve's chest like a tick burrowing under skin, incessant and in need of immediate attention. As Maeve forced herself to slow down, the feeling quickly morphed into righteous indignation about the situation at hand. Her voice rang with passionate fury, growing louder and louder with every word. "So let me get this straight. This abomination has been feeding off the souls of sacrificed women for at least a decade, using a hidden portal to literal Hell in the woods. He has killed my mother and poor Mr. Dickenson. And you want to what, research? I think we need to confront him before he can hurt anyone else!"

Michael smiled, recognizing Minerva's fiery spirit reflected in their daughter. "I understand and admire your enthusiasm. But running in blindly will only serve to get us killed and possibly sever any hope Shady Grove has of breaking free of Abaddon's grip. Abaddon has made it clear he can attack us himself or send any of his legions' worth of underlings. We need to know what we're up against, so we don't just get ourselves killed."

Maeve nodded, acknowledging the wisdom of her dad's words. "Only fools rush in," she grumbled.

"Exactly. Trina is right. Someone is aiding Abaddon. I think we need to take a cold, hard look at the facts, look up whatever demonology we can, and try to see who among our neighbors could be the culprit."

Maeve gulped. As much as she hated to admit it, Michael and Trina were right. Someone in town was willingly aiding and abetting a demon in ritual sacrifice. "I have an idea," she said. Michael nodded, encouraging her to open up. "We really didn't know much until I found *Incantations of Blood*. I think we should go back to the library. Maybe they have security cameras or something. Someone wanted me to find that book. The question is, was that someone out to warn me, or harm me?"

"Yes, a very astute observation. Let's go to the library first thing in the morning." They walked back toward the Grahams, hashing out a rough plan as they went, when they heard a fresh round of fear-filled screaming coming from inside. Without thoughts of her own safety, Maeve rushed in, not even registering the fact that the door was unlocked.

Mrs. Graham lay inside, curled in the fetal position with her hands over her face in an attempt to shield herself. Shards of shattered picture frame glass lay around her like a blanket of glittering jagged snow. "Mrs. Graham!" Maeve stopped at the edge of the sea of glass, pausing to take in her surroundings. It looked like every picture frame in the house had been thrown at the older woman, the photos hidden under the deadly shards. Black splatter glistened upon the glass. *I wonder if this is where that other demon went?*

Michael and Trina thundered into the house right behind her, their footsteps shattering the eerie quiet that followed the screams. "Who did this?" boomed Michael in dismay. Mrs. Graham remained immobile, not so much as a whimper passing her lips as fresh blood seeped through her fingers from a wound to her temple, barely visible through her splayed fingers. "Hang on, Mrs. Graham," Michael soothed as he worked his way cautiously over the remnants of the photo frames. "She's alive, just frightened and injured," he called back to Maeve and Trina.

"Michael, we don't know who, or what for that matter, did this. We need to search the house," barked Trina. Michael nodded grimly. He unsheathed his knife and stood, carefully avoiding the shards of glass. Trina handed one of her knives to Maeve. "You and I can check upstairs since you know the layout. Michael can guard Carol." Maeve nodded, gripping her weapon tightly. *I'm more likely to cut myself than I am to hurt something else.*

The women crept up the stairs, pausing and listening every few steps for any sign of movement from above. The house remained silent as a tomb. Maeve used her cell phone as a flashlight once they made it upstairs. Her room and the bathroom were clear, but the Grahams' bedroom told a different story. The room had been ransacked, an unknown number of demons wreaking havoc on everything they could find.

Claws had left the curtains in tatters, letting moonlight bathe the scene in a haunting monochrome. The bedspread had fared no better. It was shredded, feathers falling from the tears like blood from a wound, with more scattered throughout the room. A set of deep grooves were scored through the mattress. The lamps were knocked over, shades lopsided, and their bulbs shattered upon the ground. The bedside tables had toppled over, spilling their contents aimlessly. The floor-length mirror was cracked, reflecting back countless snippets of the scene. The armoire had its drawers open and askew. Papers and photographs, along with jewelry and feathers from the bedspread, littered the floor. "I'm going to take a look," whispered Maeve.

Cautiously, she entered the room. She glanced around, expecting danger in every shadowy corner. Thankfully, whoever had created this mess had fled. Maeve knelt, using her phone's flashlight to illuminate some of the scattered pages. "Trina," she gasped. "These are love letters to Mr. Graham, or should I say Ronnie, but not from Mrs. Graham." Trina sucked in a breath. "Whoever she is, she's smart enough not to sign her name. Only an initial-S." Maeve thought back to the woman she'd seen at the vigil with the white pantsuit. *It has to be her! But who is she?*

Suddenly, Trina was beside her, rifling through the letters as well. "S could be anyone, but these letters have dates. This has been going on a long time." *3-25-2011, Rachel would've still been here when her dad started this affair.* "Twelve years is a long affair. And we can't be sure this is everything. This could go back even further. Look, the more recent ones are written on stationery from the college. I wonder if they work together?"

The letters seemed to show a growing relationship. The oldest ones were hastily scrawled snippets on notebook paper in different colored inks, evolving into flowing notes on college stationery. "Trina, I think...I think she was young when it started."

"What do you mean?"

"These first ones...they almost remind me of how my peers would write in high school. The bright colored ink, the exaggerated loops on the letters...Look, she even signs the i in Ronnie with a heart. Maybe it was one of his students, a college freshman possibly, and it evolved?"

"Gross as it is, that would make sense. He definitely seems the type to not have any qualms about using his status to get what he wants." Trina gagged. "Ok, now I need to get THAT mental image out of my head."

Maeve grimaced, bile rising in her throat as she too, thought of Mr. Graham having extra-marital relations. *Abuser. Cheater. Groomer. Oh God! Ronnie! He brought her here yesterday!* Mr. Graham's crimes were mounting, and she despised him more and more with each passing moment. He would pay for all the harm he had caused, both physical and emotional. He'd been playing the long con, and his time was up.

Michael called from below, "Are you ladies ok?" The women grabbed the letters, stuffing what they could into Maeve's bag. When they returned, Michael was bent over

Mrs. Graham. "Her breathing is labored, and she's unresponsive. I think we can surmise from the claw marks around the house and the black goo on the floor that she was attacked by a demon. We really need to get her out of here before they decide to come back and finish the job." Maeve nodded.

"I'll go get my herbs now. She's in need of some serious healing, and I don't think Abaddon is done tonight. I believe he's just warming up. Be safe, you two. Michael, let's meet back at your house. The wards should keep us safe while we figure out our next steps." Trina dashed out the door without waiting for a reply.

Michael reached down and gingerly gathered Mrs. Graham in his arms. "It's going to be okay, we'll get you taken care of." Her eyes stared glassily into the distance. She was alive, but it was as if her soul had left her body, simply leaving the shell behind. As Michael turned to carry Mrs. Graham to safety, Maeve noticed a series of photographs spattered with blood where the older woman had lain. She cautiously reached for them, hoping they would provide valuable clues. She then turned to follow her father, hoping that between the cover of darkness and the commotion going on at the vigil, no one would notice them carrying Mrs. Graham through town.

137

Chapter Twelve: Lost Souls

"Maeve, hon, the spare key is under Freddy," grunted Michael as he carried Mrs. Graham toward his front door.

"Under Freddy?"

"The garden gnome! Hurry, Mrs. Graham is getting heavy. It's been a long walk." Maeve sprinted to the gnome, finding the gold key taped to the underside of his little shoe. She grabbed it and quickly unlocked the door, holding it open for her dad to pass through. He took Mrs. Graham's catatonic form into the living room, where he gently laid her on his couch. He paused to observe the older woman.

"Thankfully, the only physical damage I can see is this cut to her head. It seems shallow; head wounds just bleed a lot." Maeve folded herself onto the floor by Mrs. Graham, clasping the woman's limp hand in her own.

She heard Michael moving around in the bathroom, shuffling around as he gathered some necessities. He returned with a warm washcloth, gauze, and some other medical supplies. He handed the cloth to Maeve, who dabbed at the wound while Michael set about looking through his library, obviously searching for something in particular. He mumbled to himself as he pulled books and loose pieces of parchment from the shelves.

"Aha! Here we are," he said, pulling down a large volume titled *Mystical Ailments of the Modern Age*. He began to furiously flip through when a knock sounded at the door. Michael cocked his head at the door and Maeve took the hint. He resumed scouring the book's contents as Maeve went to answer the knocking. She looked through the peephole to ensure it was Trina before swinging the door open. The woman's arms were heavily laden with bags of herbs and tools for making remedies, sachets, and poultices.

"She has a gash on her head," Maeve offered up in lieu of a greeting.

Trina huffed as the bags sagged in her arms. "That should be an easy fix. Help me with these please, Maeve."

Together, the two women carried Trina's treasure trove of remedies into the living room, where Michael was still analyzing ancient manuscripts. Trina guided Maeve through the various herbs and extracts, and the two worked together to make a poultice of witch hazel. Trina applied the remedy directly to the wound via a gauze pad. She then started on a concoction of lemon balm, turmeric, and ginger. "This will be a powerful tea to help her heal faster." She turned to Michael. "I have done what I can for her physical form. But what about her spirit? Do you have any ideas?"

Michael turned, focusing his gaze on the still form on his couch. "I took a moment to examine her while you two made the poultice. This isn't simply shock. Her breath is shallow but steady. But look..." he gently pried her eyelid open, revealing the glazed orb underneath. He shone a pinprick of light from a pen flashlight, but there was no movement. "It's like no one is home. There's no sign of a response like someone would have while sleeping." He snapped his fingers by her ear and tapped her knee, attempting to initiate any sort of reflexive action from Mrs. Graham.

"My best guess is her spirit was severed from her body by whatever demons Abaddon sent to attack her. If it wasn't for her vitals, I'd believe her to be dead. She is lost in the spirit world. Look at this." He gently tugged at her sleeve, exposing her shoulder. Her shirt was damp with demon blood. Dozens of tiny puncture marks leeched the black substance. "If she can still feel, she must be in immense pain. Trina, can you treat the poison while Maeve and I find a way to call her spirit back home? I fear time grows short. The longer her spirit remains untethered, the greater the risks. She could become possessed, or simply wander too far to be called back."

Maeve brushed tendrils of hair from Mrs. Graham's forehead. Her heart felt heavy as she reached for the pictures she had grabbed from the floor of the Grahams' home. They were all pictures of Rachel. She slipped one into Mrs. Graham's hand, hoping it would provide the woman some small modicum of subconscious comfort.

"Sad business, that was," muttered Trina as she returned with the tea.

"What business?"

"Rachel Graham, of course."

"What's so sad about leaving home? I know it's hard, but she only went to college. Honestly, I found out earlier Mr. Graham is an abusive bastard, anyway. I don't blame her for escaping. I just wish she could have taken Mrs. Graham with her."

Trina shook her head sadly, "Oh, sweetie. I'm not shocked at all about Mr. Graham. That man always knew just how to raise my hackles. Rumors have swirled about him for years, but he's charming and nothing ever stuck. But be that as it may, just because they spun a yarn for you, doesn't make it the truth. Rachel Graham went missing twelve years ago, right before she was to graduate. I thought you knew."

"Missing?" Maeve said in shock.

"Ronald Graham insisted Rachel ran away, but I never bought it. That girl and her mother were attached at the hip. Rachel never would have left her mother behind. It devastated the town. The case even inspired one of her friends to join the police force. Carol has never been the same since, but then again, who would expect her to be?"

"You don't think..." Maeve trailed off, her thoughts careening around in her head like an out-of-control carousel. "Oh, poor Mrs. Graham. All these years her husband has been taunting her with their missing daughter, just to drive the knife in deeper. It's no wonder she was so excited to have a tenant. I wonder if she knows about the affair. Or if Rachel knew?"

"If Rachel knew, that could be motive for her disappearance. Especially if your theory is right and it involved a student."

"Trina, does Dad have Wi-Fi? I want to do some digging."

Trina smiled at Maeve's use of the endearment but refrained from commenting. "Why don't you ask him?"

Like every teenager before her, Maeve threw her head back dramatically and yelled, "Ddddaaaaaadddddd!"

Michael turned from across the room, bursting into a fit of laughter. Maeve grinned self-consciously. "Sorry, I've always wanted to do that. Plus, my secret coping mechanism is I diffuse situations with bad humor." The trio shared a brief laugh before returning to the task at hand. Michael gave his daughter the desired Wi-Fi password while Trina resumed making various herbal remedies. She decided to wait on the tea. Without her body's reflexes, Mrs. Graham would not be able to swallow.

Michael pulled out yet another ancient manuscript, looking for a ritual that would allow them to reunite Mrs. Graham's spirit with her body before it became lost in the spiritual plane.

Maeve sat at her father's wooden desk, smiling at yet another picture of her parents as teenagers. She couldn't imagine how hard it had been for Minerva to leave and then successfully reinvent herself. *You were so brave, Mom...strong too. I wish you could see me now.* Shaking her head to reorient herself to her mission, Maeve began to search. It didn't take long before she hit paydirt. "Guys, come here now!" The adults rushed over, crowding around Maeve to see what she had found.

"I was able to access NamUs, the national database of missing persons, and look! Over the past forty years, there have been at least nineteen missing women from within a fifteen-mile radius of Shady Grove."

"How has law enforcement not picked up on this?" Michael demanded. "That is too many for an area this small, even over that long of a time period." Maeve continued to scroll, taking in the ever-growing list of names: Celia Dickenson, Amanda Corey, Tayla Whittmer, Antonia Roberts, Marie Weber, Rachel Graham. The list went on and on.

"Over this time frame, law enforcement probably didn't pick up on a pattern simply because enough could be chalked up to being runaways or simply wanting to escape the small-town life. And especially in the pre-internet age, it was a lot easier to disappear and reinvent yourself. Most of them were between sixteen and twenty-four, the prime age to be missed, but also easily forgotten," Trina observed.

"Look at the dates. 2022, 2020, 2017, 2012, 2009, 2003, 1996, 1990...they were pretty far apart but suddenly grew closer and closer together. What do we think caused this?" asked Maeve. She was equal parts proud of her amateur sleuthing skills and terrified of what the results meant.

"*Esurit*," mumbled Michael.

"Gesundheit," snickered Maeve.

"I'm serious, Maeve, it's Latin. I found it written under a drawing of the portal in *Incantations of Blood*. It translates loosely to 'it hungers.' Assuming there are no other family offshoots that I know about, the last generation to have been able to have a D'Arcy sacrifice would have been my grandmother's. And she did have a sister disappear, so we can safely assume what happened to her. But my mom's generation was her and two brothers, my uncles. They both left town and didn't have any kids. Mom died in childbirth, not in Abaddon's pit. I think the portal is hungry for D'Arcy blood, and since it can't have it, it needs more frequent sacrifices."

Maeve's blood ran cold. No wonder Abaddon had honed in on her as soon as she had arrived in town, completely unaware of the consequences. She was lucky to be alive. But there was no time for self-pity. They needed to find a way to save the town. "Okay, Dad, Trina, what we need to do is figure out who has been in Shady Grove during this time. We could pull property records, but I figure you may have an idea."

"We'll burn the midnight oil and cross reference whatever records we can find. I have a suspicion, but I refuse to name anyone until we have confirmation." Michael paused while putting his arm around his daughter. "Trina will tend to Mrs. Graham and do property research. I'll look through *Incantations of Blood* to see if any of the spells and rituals explain how to stop Abaddon.

Alain may have been one owner, but that book is ancient. Probably gifted to the bastard by Abaddon himself."

The ramifications of that sunk in. They possessed a demonic grimoire tied to their bloodline. A demon was after her, eagerly awaiting her as a sacrifice. The thought chilled her to the bone. "Okay, and what do you need from me?"

Michael grimaced. "It's dangerous, but this manuscript lays out how to reunite Mrs. Graham's soul with her body. You will need to astral project and summon your mom to you. Together, the two of you will go into the spirit world and find Carol, then bring her back to us. Otherwise, we risk her becoming lost forever."

Maeve blanched. "But Dad, nothing good has happened to me there! I thought you guys wanted me to stop astral projecting?"

"If we want to save Carol, I'm afraid we have no choice. There are other methods, but they are more intricate, time-consuming, and above our ability level. Trina may be a powerful mystic and healer, and I know some Latin, but we are not priests or shamans. We are confined within our limits. Please, Maeve, Carol needs you."

As much as Maeve wanted to resist, she knew Michael was right. Trina had already applied holy water to the wound, hoping it would cleanse it like the snake bite. It had smoldered, the ichor slowly turning into normal blood, but still, Mrs. Graham had not made a sound. Her body was here, but her spirit was elsewhere. Maeve nodded. *I'm coming, Mrs. Graham.*

Michael clapped his hands together. "Let us begin."

He made a pallet of blankets on the floor as Trina hurriedly smudged the room, hoping to ward off any lingering demonic presence. Maeve removed her protective sachet, feeling naked without its comforting warmth. Fear coursed through her veins. *I have to do this. I have to...for Mrs. Graham.* Michael carefully laid Mrs. Graham on the floor, resting her head gently on a pillow. Maeve lay beside her, grasping her lifeless hand. Trina set up candles and crystals around the room, similar to what they had used earlier during the seance.

"Drink this tea. It will put you into a meditative trance that should trigger the astral projection. Your dad and I will be here, able to wake you if it appears you are in danger. I also put some herbs for protection in. We will keep you safe, Maeve. I promise." Maeve drank the tea, not stopping to ask what herbs Trina had used. Time was of the essence. She laid back against the pillows, letting Trina's lilting voice soothe her into the promised trance. Before long, she felt the familiar feeling of being out of her body.

This time, she was in control. She hung in the air, directly above her body. She closed her eyes and drew in a deep breath. *Focus. I need to find Mom.* She went to the window, determined to start her exploration. Outside, she heard the screams that had haunted her to the core since her previous visits to the lagoon. Her heart broke as the legion of tortured souls cried out for mercy from their eternal torment. Against the backdrop of pain and suffering, she made out a softer, yet more urgent sound. In the distance, Mrs. Graham was calling for Rachel.

She sounded like she was in the direction of the forest. Maeve didn't want to go there, afraid Abaddon might snatch her very soul. But she could hear the spirit crying out, begging for her long-lost daughter, to no avail. *I have to try.* Cautiously, she approached the forest; the grass tickling her bare feet. Similar to the dream with Celia, a figure emerged from the treeline. Only this time, it was Minerva.

"Maeve," whispered Minerva, her voice catching in her throat. She flew across the distance, almost tackling her daughter into an embrace. "Oh, sweetheart." The two held on to one another for dear life, tears streaming down both their faces. "I see you opened my Pandora's box of secrets." Minerva stroked Maeve's long hair as she took in her daughter. "I'm so sorry. I thought we would have more time for me to tell you everything. I never wanted you to find out like this. I never meant to leave you."

"Oh Mom, I know. I've missed you." Maeve clung to her mother, relishing the feel of a hug she never thought she would experience again. "Mom, I need your help. Someone is helping Abaddon, and they hurt my friend Mrs. Graham. She's out wandering the spirit world, alone and defenseless."

Minerva pulled away, looking Maeve up and down. "You've grown since I last saw you. You're stronger, wiser, and braver. Come, we will find this lost soul and return her, and you, to the mortal plane before Abaddon can get his claws into you."

Chapter Thirteen: A Mother's Love

Minerva grabbed Maeve's hand, and together, they entered the forest. Minerva deftly led them through the beech trees, filtering through as if she had every twist of the maze committed to memory. "I'm so sorry for all of this, Maeve. I've been watching over you every day since I died. I didn't want you to need me, but I wanted to be here in case you did." Maeve squeezed Minerva's hand three times, their secret sign for I love you.

"Why did you come back to Shady Grove, Mom? You spent so much time away, it had to have been hard. Did you know about Abaddon?" The trees were getting thicker, the tormented souls louder. And amidst it all, Mrs. Graham could still be heard screaming for her daughter.

"I felt awful for the Dickensons. I thought about what I would ever do if something happened to you. I didn't know what I was getting into. I thought it was safe…as long as I didn't bring you." She hung her head, regret evident on her face. "I'm so glad you found your dad. Michael was the only man I ever loved. Tell him I'm sorry, and I never stopped loving him." She squeezed Maeve's hand three times as well.

"I will, Mom. Wait!" She pulled her mom down, hard. They crashed into the ground, Maeve's knees stinging with the impact. The demon from her bedroom window hurtled above them before circling back to face them. Mother and daughter prepared to face him. A demon had separated them once before; it would not happen again.

The demon soared above the trees; the women following in rapid pursuit. The spiritual plane had some advantages. Fighting in the air would give them more space than fighting in the forest. Maeve would just need to avoid a nasty fall. The demon turned, tucking his wings in for a rapid dive. Maeve remembered Trina's knife. She grabbed it, waiting until the demon was upon her before thrusting it. Her aim was true.

Maeve's blade was coated in gore, the demon's eye pierced on the tip. The demon shrieked, grasping at his ruined eye socket. Minerva began to chant in Latin, struggling to be heard over the creature. He made to lunge again, only to come up short. Minerva had created a force field around the women. "Leave now, and I will grant you mercy. Aim for my daughter again, and I will send your maimed remains to Lucifer." She glared at the creature, who cowered in pain and fear. With a pop, he disappeared back to whence he came, determined to live another day.

From their vantage point in the sky, the duo could more easily hear Mrs. Graham. "Let's go Maeve. That demon will come back with help." Hand in hand they flew, honing in on Mrs. Graham's cries. The woman was hysterical now, her continued pleas for her missing daughter going unanswered. They found the poor woman wandering around in the woods, screaming until her throat was raw and she was gasping for breath. "Rachel..." she rasped. *A mother's love really is limitless...*

Minerva descended, stretching out her hand to the woman. "Please, Mrs. Graham, let me help you." But Mrs. Graham shook her head.

"My bastard of a husband said she was here! This is where he took her. I have ta find her! My baby girl, my Rachel!" Fresh sobs wracked the woman's fragile frame and Maeve felt her heart break. She too descended.

"Please Mrs. Graham, this is my mom. She was a medium before she died. She can help find Rachel if she is actually dead. But for now, we have to get you help."

Mrs. Graham sniffled, taking in the woman before her. "Well, I declare! You're Maeve's mama?" Minerva nodded. "I reckon you understand. I can't just leave my baby out here all alone. She could be just over yonder. I can't give up on her."

This time Minerva firmly grasped the woman, pulling her along. "I understand, I really do. I died trying to help the Dickensons find their daughter. Now, it is my turn to help you. But, you have to return to your body. Your spirit is in danger here, and your body is in danger as well." Mrs. Graham blanched.

"Please, Mrs. Graham. You were attacked. We have to get you back to your body before another demon finds us. Or worse, finds your body unattended. You could become possessed and be unable to return to the land of the living."

"But my baby..."

"I will scour the entire spirit realm for her, but please. You have to go. NOW!" The sound of beating wings rang out in the distance. Minerva turned, fear in her eyes. "Not today. Not my daughter." She turned to Maeve and Mrs. Graham. "There's no time to do this gently. Maeve," she looked at her daughter, "I love you." Without warning, she put a hand on each woman's chest and shoved, forcing them back into their physical forms.

Mrs. Graham shot upright, gasping for air as her spirit melded back into place. "Whoa, whoa Mrs. Graham, careful now!" exclaimed Trina. The older woman took a few shuddering breaths and things settled down internally. "Deep breaths, yes, just like that. Can you tell us what happened to you?"

Mrs. Graham looked around, attempting to take stock of her surroundings. "Where am I? I'm plumb tired."

Michael stepped forward. "My home, Mrs. Graham. We were walking Maeve to your house when we heard a scream. We found you lying in a sea of shattered glass and photographs of your daughter."

Mrs. Graham moaned, the pain returning to her head and to her heart. "'He... he told me she was dead."

"Who, Mrs. Graham?"

"My husband! He came home for lunch and flew into a mighty rage. I took his special book a couple a days ago. I refused to admit it to him and he made me pay for it."

"Wait, special book?" Maeve asked, even though she already had a feeling she knew what the woman was talking about.

Mrs. Graham looked at her and smiled weakly. " I think you're well acquainted with it now. It's called *Incantations of Blood*."

Maeve gasped. "You put that in my bag?"

"I did. A whole hill a beans of good it did me. My husband told me there was a curse on the town. He said my blood is special... something about my bloodline. But he also said it wasn't me he wanted. It was Rachel."

"Who is he, Mrs. Graham?"

Tears ran from the older woman's face. "I...I'm not sure. I didn't use to believe in the supernatural, but now... you saw what happened to me. I think my husband is cavorting with demons. And I think he used our daughter to do it. Oh, my poor sweet girl. I should have left him years ago. This is all my fault. I always said that it'll all come out in the wash, but I don't think it will this time."

Trina wrapped her arms around Mrs. Graham as the woman's body convulsed from over a decade of pent-up anguish and despair. She rocked back and forth, wailing to the sky, "Rachel, my baby. Rachel!" Maeve reached over and held Mrs. Graham as well.

"Is lunch when he gave you the black eye?"

"Yes, he thought he had misplaced the book, but when it was gone, he knew I'd taken it. He just kept shouting that I didn't know what I was doing, and I was just a spiteful bitch. Funny how he would expect anything less. A course, I'm spiteful."

"Understandable," Trina murmured. "We're glad to have you back, Mrs. Graham. I think we have some things to discuss."

Michael interjected, "You said your husband mentioned bloodline...I think we may be related. You see, my family has a curse. There's a demon after us, tied to the town. If you're one of us..." Michael trailed off, hesitant to reveal too much and shock the woman.

"I've withstood a demon attack, my soul went a wandering, and Maeve's mama just pushed me back into my body. Gimme a minute, and I think we can talk this through. I just need to catch my breath."

Trina took the opportunity to offer Mrs. Graham her herbal tea, which the older woman accepted gratefully. The two women fell into a whispered conversation, leaving Maeve and Michael to have a heartfelt chat.

"Dad, Mom wanted me to tell you something." Michael froze, not sure he wanted to know. "She... she told me she loves you and she's sorry."

"I forgive her, Maeve. I loved your mother; no other woman could ever hold a candle to her. And now, she has given me the greatest gift I never expected to receive, you," he said as he gently cupped her chin. "I will protect you, to my dying breath." Michael joined the women on the floor as Mrs. Graham continued weeping, gradually turning to bouts of hiccupping sobs, and finally, nothing.

Slowly, she raised her head, a new steel glinting in her gaze. "My bastard of a husband is working with a demon. I'm pretty sure he sacrificed his own flesh and blood; and what? I will end him."

Michael shook her hand. "Welcome to the team, Mrs. Graham. I think after all of this, it's time to get some food. Maeve, while you were gone, Trina and I found some information. Let's eat, and we can discuss the next steps. I think we're closing in on some critical answers."

"Ok, let's go." Together they stood and loaded into Michael's car, driving across town to Steven's, the best diner in Indiana.

Chapter Fourteen: Just an Indiana Night

Michael stopped in front of a quintessential 50s-style diner, lit up with classic neon pink and aqua. Painted silhouettes of people dancing lined the walls, harking back to the days of hand jives and sock hops. "Good Golly, Miss Molly" blasted from the jukebox in the corner as the group found a booth. They settled in and a pretty waitress with a pink poodle skirt and white roller-skates zoomed over.

"Welcome to Steven's; my name is Danielle. May I take your order or do you need a minute to look at the menu?" Without hesitation, Michael ordered four tenderloins, two orders of deep-fried pickles, two orders of breaded mushrooms, an entire bottle of ranch dressing, and four bottomless root beer floats. As the waitress zoomed off, Maeve sighed. *Tenderloin, ranch, and root beer...it doesn't get more small-town Indiana than this.* Michael's voice cut into her thoughts.

"Ok, let's get down to business. Carol, please tell us what you know."

Mrs. Graham began to unravel her family's mysteries... "Ronald never hit me when Rachel was home. But after she disappeared, it was like he blamed me. Up until his outburst, I never suspected him of having anything to do with Rachel's disappearance, or demons for that matter." She paused, steeling herself against the grief and instead choosing to focus on her rage.

"Is he a piece of shit? Oh Lord, yes. Did I ever think him a danger to anyone but me? No. But lately...he started acting odd. I caught him a couple a times, murmuring into a black book about 'finding the last of the bloodline' and 'necessary sacrifices.' I just thought he was finally going off his rocker, maybe one a those newfangled STIs. I suspected an affair a couple of times, but whoever it was, he hid it well. I could never find evidence. But as the years went on, he continued to pull away, which is odd considering the lengths he went to find me."

Trina's ears perked up at the odd choice of words. "What do you mean to find you?"

"Well dearie, in hindsight, it's like he sought me out. I was living down south in Louisiana when he came to my hometown. He was a tall drink of iced tea...had all the girls fawning over him. But he only had eyes for me. I was smitten, and right after I turned eighteen, we got married and moved here to his hometown. I always asked why he was visiting and he would always reply he was looking for a southern bell to tame his heart. Then he'd laugh and say he got himself some whiskey in a teacup. Things used to be good between us. I don't know where I went so wrong."

Trina gazed solemnly. "You didn't do anything wrong. He did. He lied, cheated, and beat you. And that's just what we can confirm. Your only fault is loving the wrong man. He committed crimes against that trust; you didn't do anything."

A tear slid down Mrs. Graham's cheek. "I thought I could fix him...fix us. But now that he's shown his true colors, I see all the signs I missed. There is no more us. He took everything from me and I'm going to make him pay."

Maeve cut in awkwardly. "Mrs. Graham, why did you put the book in my bag?"

"I noticed Ronald getting more agitated the closer it came to your arrival. He was acting downright strange the day you arrived. Normally he doesn't give two shakes of a tail feather about guests, but he was positively giddy that you were coming." She paused sheepishly. "Honestly, at first I worried you might be the pretty peach that'd caught his eye. But when I met you, I knew that wasn't the case. Still, it was strange. He was so put out when you slept through dinner your first night. I'd never seen him like that. I caught him late at night, mumbling into the book, and I decided that somehow, it was connected to you. I tried to open it, but it gave off a real menacing air. I knew something was up. I followed you to the library and slipped it into your bag, knowing I had already directed you to Trina's shop. I hoped y'all could put together whatever puzzle pieces I was missing." She put a hand to her black eye. "I just never expected him to attack me over it. Up 'til today, he was always so careful not to leave visible marks. After losing the book, he came unglued. It was sick, getting beat at lunch and then having to act like everything was ok at dinner. I haven't seen Ronald since, though. It was a demon that attacked me and destroyed my house."

Maeve placed a comforting hand on Mrs. Graham's shoulder. "He is never going to lay a finger on you again."

"Oh dearie, I know. If he tries, I'll end him. If he really did harm my Rachel, there's nothing holding me back now. I have no remaining family, nothing to live for. I'm madder than a wet hen."

They were interrupted by Danielle arriving with their order, tenderloin and sides coming in paper versions of classic cars. "Eat up, loves! I'll be back soon to see if anyone needs a fresh float!"

The table dissolved into a chorus of lip-smacking and sucking straws as the group dove into their midwestern feast. "Ok," Michael began through bites of crispy, juicy tenderloin, "*Incantations of Blood* did indeed contain some rituals and spells. Most of it is for dark wizards, things way too advanced for us to even attempt. Plus, most of it is meant to cause harm. However, I did find how to sever the curse."

"You did!?!" all three women asked in unison.

"I did. It's pretty straightforward, thankfully, but Abaddon isn't going to let us do it easily. We have to go to the lagoon and offer up D'Arcy blood while renouncing our family's ties to Abaddon. Doing so will banish him back to Hell, and cut off the lagoon. Here, let me show you."

He opened the book to the back, where borderline illegible scrawl covered every inch of the pages. "Here," he pointed. "Allow me to read D'Arcy's awful handwriting. 'Abaddon revealed to me the greatest secret of all. His magic is anchored to this town, my bloodline acting as the standard against which the town is weighed. If it were to die out, Abaddon could move on, or choose a new liege. Conversely, if my line wishes, they may end the transactional nature of the curse. One or more of my line must go to Abaddon's secret place and offer their blood, while using his language to sever the ties I have created. The demon will be freed from this place and forced to return to Hell where God intended him to reside.' Heavy stuff here, ladies."

"Ok Dad, so what's the plan exactly? Me and you sneak off to this 'secret place' while Trina and Mrs. Graham play defense? That has to be the lagoon, right?"

"Definitely the lagoon, once we can figure out how to get there. But no honey, not just us. Carol too. From what Mr. Graham was saying, I think it's safe to assume she is also of D'Arcy blood. I'm guessing an offshoot from my mom's generation. From what I can tell, a sacrifice is supposed to happen before the age of twenty-five. The only exception being Alain's wife, which started this whole mess, to begin with."

"That makes sense, Michael. Like I said, I was from outta town and Ronald insisted we move here to his hometown. It's always been strange. I never knew what the black droplets that would randomly appear were. But after my attack, I know them to be demon blood. I was only eighteen when we got married and Ronald was insistent we have a baby immediately. He had to have already been in league with this Abaddon. Sounds like he hunted me down to make a new crop of D'Arcy's for Abaddon to mine for blood. Jokes on Ronald, though, bless his heart. He had a low sperm count. It took years to get pregnant with Rachel. I was twenty-six by then."

Michael nodded in acknowledgment. "That explains why he spared you. Assuming Ronald is indeed in cahoots with Abaddon, they probably wanted you to make the next generation of D'Arcy sacrifices before offing you. Inadvertently, Ronald and his worthless prick saved your life."

Mrs. Graham laughed, shooting root beer out of her nose. "Owww, owww that burns! That might be the only worthwhile thing his prick ever did. We had to go to a clinic to get help conceiving Rachel so I'm not even going to give him credit for that." Tears formed as she remembered her daughter. "I just can't believe he killed her. It's like trying to wrap my mind around a greased pig. To hurt his own daughter...She was his pride and joy. And for what? What is he getting out of this?"

"Power maybe? Status? Wealth? Who knows, maybe he's just one of those guys that likes to do a bit of dirty work to feel important," Maeve interjected, angry at the man who had hurt so many innocent people. "Maybe it has something to do with his affair? After your attack, we found love letters dating back to 2011. It looks like it's still going on." Maeve retrieved the letters from her bag. "I don't want to hurt you, but could you look at the handwriting? Maybe you'll recognize it."

Mrs. Graham nodded, accepting several of the proffered slips of paper. She gasped, flipping back and forth between the pages as if the answer would somehow miraculously change. "Yes...yes, I would know this handwriting anywhere."

"Who is it, Carol?" Trina asked.

The older woman took a big gulp, trying to remove the lump of disgust in her throat. "Well, we can add predator to the list. S is Scheana, and from the looks a these letters, this started all the way back in 2009. She would have only been fifteen. That disgusting pig! His own daughter's best friend! I'm just so torn up!" Her eyes flashed with newfound hatred as the group took in the news.

"Mrs. Graham, do you think Rachel knew?"

"Oh my God! Maybe that's what happened! If she found out...he might have sacrificed her not only to appease Abaddon, but to save his sorry ass."

Michael nodded solemnly. "That does seem on par with his character, or lack thereof. What matters now is..." A sudden blaring silenced the group. Across their phones was a matching text message, pumping a fresh wave of adrenaline into their veins.

AMBER ALERT: MISSING FROM SHADY GROVE, IN: MCKINLEY SUMMERS, AGE 17

"He took another girl!" exclaimed Trina. "Okay, people, chop chop." She clapped her hands, snapping those assembled to attention. "We now know the following pieces of information. An ancient abyss linked to Hell resides hidden in the trees of Shady Grove, an abyss that can only be sated by either the ancestral blood of the D'Arcy line or those they choose to sacrifice. Michael and Maeve, and apparently Mrs. Graham, are the only remaining D'Arcy's. Mr. Graham has, for reasons unknown, been aiding the demon Abaddon in his sacrifice of young women. And now another girl has been taken. Did I miss anything?"

Everyone sat for a moment in stunned silence before Maeve piped up. "I know where to find the lagoon."

"How?" exclaimed Michael.

Maeve simply held up her hand with the mark that Celia had branded upon her. "We follow Celia's path." The group immediately swirled into motion. They knew not what they would face, but no one could deny the pressing sense of urgency and destiny that had descended upon them.

Chapter Fifteen: Have Mercy

Armed with flashlights, herbs and potions from Tri-na, holy water from Michael's stash, knives that Michael had blessed with Latin prayers, *Incantations of Blood*, and a heaping amount of rage, the group set out for the woods. Maeve led the way, her chest ablaze with a white-hot passion. How dare Mr. Graham hurt his wife, murder his own daughter and countless others, and take yet another victim? She was going to make him pay. They parked on the edge of the treeline. Unbeknownst to them, it was the exact spot Celia parked in the previous year. Their car doors sounded like a firing squad as they were slammed shut. The group didn't care about being quiet. Abaddon knew they were on their way. They were ready to take the fight for their town, and for their lives, straight to him.

The crisp grass crunched under their feet as they approached the trees. *This is just like my dreams.* Maeve's mark stung as a matching sigil became visible on one of the beech trees. "We go in here. Is everyone ready?" Michael, Trina, and Mrs. Graham all nodded their assent.

As Maeve took her first step into the woods, the usual chatter of a forest at night tapered away into an eerie, unnatural silence. The air practically shimmered with the promise of fresh spilled blood. Maeve Baudelaire and Carol Graham, the last remaining ancestral daughters of Shady Grove, had come to break a centuries-old oath sworn in blood and suffering. Crossing the tree line ignited the mark on Maeve's hand with an ethereal, fiery glow. "Over here," whispered Michael. Several feet into the densely packed stretch of trees, a matching mark ignited on yet another tree trunk.

"Celia's path," Maeve declared. Maeve led the way, her father at her heels, followed by a newly determined Mrs. Graham, with Trina and her bag of herbs and potions bringing up the rear. A harsh cackle cut the still night air. Mrs. Graham threw on her flashlight just in time to illuminate the winged demon from Maeve's most recent astral projection. This time, he wasn't alone.

Vengeance was written across the demon's face as his one good eye fixated on Maeve. Four more demons, smaller but of a similar build, fanned out around him. "So the fight begins," Michael murmured. The demons flew into motion, beating their wings and wildly slinging their claws. Maeve cried out as she suffered a devastating gash to her shoulder and down her left arm. The demon reared to strike again, but Maeve didn't give him a chance. One quick swing of her knife hacked off his hand.

Mrs. Graham took on two, her mama bear instincts in full effect. She sliced the throat of one as it approached, leaving her going toe to toe with the second-largest winged devil. He sized her up, looking for weak points. "I can still hear your daughter's screams. Her pain is delicious..."

She screamed while her blade zinged through the air but came up short as the demon flew away. Instead, he reared at Michael, whose back was turned as he and Trina faced the remaining demons.

"Dad, look out!"

"Ahhh!" The winged beast sank his claws into Michael's shoulder blades as he lifted the man from the ground, intent on carrying him off.

"Not on my watch!" Trina threw a vial of holy water into the demon's triumphant face. He crashed to the ground, screaming and thrashing wildly. Michael's back was shredded as the demon flailed. Finally, his corporeal form dissolved, leaving a blood-soaked Michael face down in the dirt.

"Dad!" *No no no no! I can't lose him, too. I just found him!*

"No time; there's still three of them." Trina ushered the women into a circle, their weapons ready as the demons circled overhead. The one whom Maeve had fought earlier lunged again, but he too got a face full of holy water. From the ground, Michael held up a shaking hand. He pointed at the remaining two demons, chanting in Latin. Without warning, the two figures exploded, raining rancid carnage down upon the women.

The group paused, their hearts beating out of their chests from the fight. "Maeve, Michael, let me tend to your wounds." Trina pulled some bandages and poultices from her pack. "Abaddon is determined to give us a fight. Maybe we should proceed a little more cautiously." She bandaged Maeve first. "You're going to need stitches, but this is what I can do for now."

She turned to Michael, sucking in a breath at his exposed back. "Oh..."

"That bad, T?"

"Michael, it's really, really bad." Blood and ichor seeped from the wounds, exposing bits of muscle at the deepest cuts. "I'll do what I can, but you are in desperate need of medical attention." She helped Michael remove his shirt, then quickly cleansed the wound with holy water. "Carol, help me." Together, the two women wrapped Michael's entire back. "Move cautiously; you are at severe risk for blood loss."

"Thank you, Trina, Carol. But we must press on." He drew himself up, grimacing with pain. Maeve cautiously approached and gave him a gentle hug. "We must continue, no matter what Abaddon throws our way. I'm sure that was just the welcome brigade."

This time, they moved deliberately and stealthily. They were determined not to shatter the perverse quiet of the forest. Every few feet, just as the group felt they had lost the trail, a new mark would illuminate upon a trunk, lighting their way bit by bit through the fall foliage. Slowly, the usual forest scents gave way to the rank stench of decomposition mixed with the copper tang of blood.

"Oh shit," grumbled Michael.

The tortured wails of hundreds of souls cascaded over the group with the force of a hurricane, cutting to the very essence of their being. "We're close," Maeve uttered with the determination of a young woman with fire in her blood. A gunshot ripped through the night, the bullet zipping right past Maeve's right ear before implanting itself into the withered bark of a nearby beech tree.

"Stop right there!" boomed the distinct voice of Ronald Graham.

Maeve, Michael, and Trina froze. They had expected a demon, but somehow had not expected a madman with a shotgun. Carol Graham, however, was over her husband's bullshit. "Ronald Eustace Graham, I don't know who in the almighty blazing hells you think you are, but I am not having it."

The sound of the shotgun reloading reverberated through the forest, sending the group into a flurry of action. Mrs. Graham stood her ground, years of pent-up frustration finally boiling over, igniting the short woman with indignant, righteous fury. "You listen to me, Ronald. I have put up with you long enough! You laid hands on me too many times to count, and I never spoke an ill word about you. But you just had to go for Rachel. And then I find out you've been sleeping with Scheana, your own daughter's best friend! How long Ronald? Since she was a teenager?"

The man paused, obviously startled that his wife had figured out the identity of his mistress. "I never did anything to that girl that she didn't want. Why, she still takes my cock every chance she can get. Maeve almost caught us yesterday. Her favorite spot is our bed, where she can fantasize about taking everything from you. Just like she took Rachel."

Mrs. Graham froze. "Just like she did WHAT?"

"You heard me, you old bitch. Rachel was always the best of us. It pained me that I was going to have to sacrifice her. But in the end, she made it easy. Scheana got sloppy, and Rachel caught us. She said she was going to go to tell you...that I would lose everything and that Scheana was nothing but a home-wrecking whore."

Mrs. Graham grimaced. If there was one thing she remembered about Scheana, it was the girl's stubborn, prideful nature.

"Rachel tried to leave, but Scheana went after her. I didn't see the start of it, but when I got there, Scheana had straddled Rachel. She was punching her again and again, screaming about how she was going to be her stepmom someday. Rachel was fighting back, pulling hair, and scratching like a jungle cat. She managed to claw Scheana across the face and knock her off of her. I...I had to stop her."

"Ronald...what did you do?"

"I put her in a chokehold. When she passed out, Scheana helped me load Rachel into the car. Together, we went to the lagoon and sacrificed Rachel. She's been helping me ever since. It's amazing what having a beautiful woman on your side can do. It's so easy for her to lure the girls here. Then we finish them off together. She even lured Celia out here last year...some text about having information about Tayla Whittmer. She stayed hidden while that girl drowned. We even had sex by the pit afterward. One of the best nights of my life, if we're being honest. I always feel so powerful after a sacrifice."

"You're a sick man. I will drag your sorry ass back to town and make sure you're ruined for life. Abuse, grooming, murder...I hope ya don't drop the soap too often in the prison showers."

"I'm going to be the next legend of this town. Alain D'Arcy may have founded this place, but I am going to revive it! Buildings will have my name and books will be written about me." He roared as he stepped out into a pale sliver of moonlight, his ego not allowing him to confront his wife from the shadows. After all, how dare she speak to him in such a manner? "I will be..." he never got to finish. Before he could blink, Mrs. Graham threw a hunting knife straight into his gut with a satisfying *THWONK*.

He screamed like a stuck pig as blood welled around the wound. Michael had circled around and tackled him, driving the knife to the hilt upon their impact with the ground. Mrs. Graham charged over like a bull seeing red as she rained blow after blow upon his head, chest, and groin. Finally, she noticed the shotgun he had dropped. As her husband grunted and squealed, she took aim.

Through his haze of pain, Mr. Graham pleaded, "Please Carol, have mercy." She leveled the gun and fired.

Chapter Sixteen: A Woman Scorned

Blood and bits of bone exploded into the night, right along with Mr. Graham's right kneecap. His shriek was loud enough to wake the dead. CLICK. Mrs. Graham reloaded. "Please… please… Carol, I've been a good husband to you all these years."

"Good husband? You were as likely to beat me as you were to look at me! You're a sorry excuse for a man!" The next shot eviscerated his other knee, ensuring that without outside aid, Mr. Graham would die in the forest, unable to even crawl for help. His screams of agony evoked nothing in his wife as she loaded the gun again. "I hate you, Ronald. I've hated you for years. I just refused to admit it to myself. I did everything for you, for us, for our family. And all you did was take and destroy." She cocked the gun toward his most precious possession, his family jewels.

"Carol, you wouldn't...." he begged in between sharp, ragged breaths of visceral pain.

"Where is Scheana? I'm assuming that she-devil is out in these infernal woods, too."

"Scheana...." he hissed as rivers of blood wept from his destroyed knees, "she won't let you get away with this. Maeve will be sacrificed...Abaddon will be pleased...he'll grant me a new body like he always has."

Mrs. Graham approached her mangled and mauled husband, the barrel of the gun still trained on his nether region. "What do you mean 'like he always has?'"

He stared at her with a wolfish grin, pain making him reckless. "I'm surprised you and your little crew haven't figured it out yet. I am Alain D'Arcy, reincarnated through the ages. Abaddon has not abandoned me yet...but without Maeve..."

"You will never take Maeve!" Mrs. Graham pulled the trigger.

A girlish scream unlike anything Ronald Graham had ever heard before emanated from his mouth, the sheer force of it blasting his throat raw like sandpaper. And yet, at the sight of what was left of his dick and balls splattered across the forest floor, he could not stop. Finally, the pain became too great for his fragile mind to handle, and he passed out.

Michael, grunting in pain, dragged Mr. Graham's limp form to the base of a large beech tree. He shook his head angrily. "I can't believe we didn't see the signs. Why else would this bumfuck hick be able to do what he does? It explains the grimoire, and even why he went out of town just to find you, Carol. There's a list of names in the back, starting with Alain and ending with Ronald. Each one of them has, to varying degrees, been an influential man in Shady Grove's history. Those must be all of Alain's identities over the years. I bet when the line started to die out, he knew he had to start over again. By marrying you, he was able to concentrate the bloodline. Too bad for him; his current form had some drawbacks."

Mrs. Graham snorted. "You mean his now-destroyed, worthless prick?"

"Yes, that."

Maeve floundered, her brain struggling to catch up to this development. "He's...he's Alain D'Arcy! But he would be...centuries old!"

Mrs. Graham scoffed, "Believe me, it ain't hard to believe. The man may be part demon himself." She spat on her husband's ruined body. "He used his good looks, his smooth-talking, and now Scheana to get close to those girls. Lord knows he could be charming when he wanted to be. But he got too big for his britches and it felt good to knock him down a couple a pegs."

Maeve moved forward, putting her hand on Mrs. Graham's shoulder. "Are you ok?"

"Honestly... yes, honey. Butter my buns and call me a biscuit. I wish I would have stood up to him a long time ago. Maybe Rachel would still be alive. I didn't know about the cheating back then, and even when I suspected him, I never knew who. I never would've guessed... And Rachel...I never suspected him, but I knew in my heart she was dead. At least...at least now I know and can make him pay for it. There will be no new body this time. As for Scheana..." she cocked the gun again, the sound a warning all its own, "she has her own sins to pay for. Hell hath no fury like a woman scorned." Placing the loaded weapon against her shoulder, Mrs. Graham took the lead as the crew, on guard against future attacks, traveled through the forest.

"I'm worried about what happens to the town when we banish Abaddon?" Trina mused.

"I've been wondering that too," Michael reflected. "*Incantations of Blood* is clear that Abaddon is anchored to the town. However, it's obvious that while he has influence through the likes of Alain, the town is still its own entity...We have to stop this, but I fear we may be creating a whole other problem for Shady Grove."

CRACK!

A branch broke to their left, causing the group to halt. The leaves began to rustle as something approached them. Mrs. Graham trained the gun into the darkness, ready to fire. A figure jumped from the darkness, aiming for her. It was Scheana, her hair tangled with leaves, her mascara running as her body shook with sobs. "Oh, Mrs. Graham, I'm so glad you're here. You won't believe..."

Mrs. Graham aimed the gun square at the younger woman's chest. "You're right; I won't believe a word outta your mouth. Ronald told me everything. You've got gumption speaking to me now. You helped kill my daughter." Scheana's eyes grew wide. Caught in the lie, she looked between the group, hoping to find someone sympathetic to her cause. When it became obvious no one was buying the shit she was selling, she dropped the act.

"I did kill your daughter, you bitch. And I'd do it again too. She got what was coming to her. I-" Mrs. Graham fired, blasting a devastating hole in Scheana's shoulder. She screamed as she fell to her knees. Her right arm grasped at the wound, as her left arm hung uselessly, the nerves damaged from the shrapnel. Her face registered pain and shock. "You...you shot me?"

"You're lucky that's all I did. The only reason you're alive is so you can tell us where the girl is." Scheana's eyes rolled back into her head and she began to shake. She spasmed as her body struggled to replace the blood that was rapidly seeping into the forest floor. Trina moved to assist, but Mrs. Graham stopped her with a raised hand. "No, there's no mercy for cold-blooded murderers. I can forgive sleeping with Ronald, that's on him. She was just a child and Lord knows he's no prize. I will never fight over a man. But killing Rachel is a sin she must pay for."

Scheana gasped, "Mercy... the girl... at... Lagoon... mercy... please."

"Carol, I can't stand by and watch her suffer." Mrs. Graham stepped aside begrudgingly as Trina moved to help. The mystic shook her head as she reached into her pack, rummaging through for her herbs. She sank to her knees beside the injured woman. "Here, let me see."

Scheana removed her hand, only to smack Trina across the face, leaving a wet, bloody handprint in her wake. "Abaddon will devour her soon. He always gets his due. And when he's finished with her, he's coming for your precious Maeve."

Trina stood, and Mrs. Graham glared at Scheana. "Stop being ugly. I can see you're still one helluva actress. But your eyes don't lie. You're afraid. You won't die from that wound, but you will suffer. Go crawl to what remains of your darling Ronnie. I can't guarantee he's still alive." Scheana stood, swaying from pain. No one moved to help her as she limped toward the forest entrance, blood dotting the forest floor as she went.

Maeve rested her head on Mrs. Graham's shoulder as the older woman sighed, her body shaking with adrenaline. "I know that was hard, but you did the right thing letting her live." A steely resolve settled onto Mrs. Graham as she stood taller.

"She's lucky I only shot her. Let's get McKinley and put an end to this cycle. Abaddon is about to learn about a whole new level of Hell...me." Mrs. Graham and Maeve led the way as the group advanced, growing closer to a fight no one was sure they would survive.

Chapter Seventeen: Centuries of Souls

They walked for an hour after their dramatic confrontation with Scheana. Maeve now led the way. Michael limped behind as his shredded back continued to bleed, Trina beside him, gazing up at the wound with worry. Mrs. Graham kept her head on a swivel, ready to blow any would-be attackers away with the shotgun. While on high alert, everyone used the unnatural quiet to process what they had learned. Rachel was dead. Alain D'Arcy was alive and had been for centuries. Scheana had been a willing accomplice in numerous murders for twelve years.

The combined stench of decomposition and coppery blood had settled onto the group like a haze of smoke. The wailing of countless tortured souls grew louder with every step. The sound burrowed its way into their psyches, promising untold pain to come. Still, they pressed on, following the trail of trees marked with Celia's glowing sign. Finally, they came to a large tree, its trunk withered with age. Ichor dripped like sap from its trunk as the sigil glowed from the center.

"Is that-?" Maeve was cut off as a glowing figure emerged from the shadows. "MOM!"

"Hello, sweetheart, Trina, Michael...Carol, I found someone you've been looking for." She stretched her hand out, ushering another glowing figure out of the darkness.

Mrs. Graham let out a shout. "RACHEL! Oh, my baby..." Rachel flew to her mom, her spiritual form not allowing them to embrace. "Oh sweetie, I'm so sorry. I should have left town with you and never looked back. To think, your own father-"

"Shhhh, Mom. You couldn't have known. No one could have. I don't know if he would have if I hadn't discovered what he was up to with...her." She turned, pointing into the trees. Mrs. Graham picked up the shotgun and aimed right as Scheana stumbled through the trees.

Mrs. Graham leveled the gun, revenge in her eyes. "I gave you your chance, Scheana. This time I won't be so generous." The injured woman let out a hideous cackle as her skin split, revealing black scales. The skin fell away, leaving a demonic snake, bigger than the last, in her wake. *Not again,* thought Maeve.

"Abaddon hassss blesssssssed me. I have been reborn!" Scheana lunged, aiming right for Mrs. Graham. Rachel stepped in front of her mother, raising her hand. Scheana slammed against an invisible barrier mere centimeters from Rachel's outstretched fingertips.

"These souls are under my protection. It's nice to see you in your true form, Scheana. Being a snake suits you."

"Thisss issn't over! Abaddon will not let you-" She cut off with a scream as Mrs. Graham fired, the shot blowing away part of Scheana's reptilian face. Out of ammo, Mrs. Graham dropped the gun. She lunged forward, slamming her knife into Scheana's soft underbelly. The blade sank to the hilt as black ooze poured from the wound. Scheana's body spasmed as Mrs. Graham removed the knife, stabbing in a frenzy until the snake lay still, black blood leaching into the ground like an oil spill. Mrs. Graham smiled.

"I hope she rots in Hell like she deserves."

Maeve shook as reality set in. *Mrs. Graham killed a woman! Demons are one thing…but Scheana was a person, once.* Michael solemnly put his hand on his daughter's shoulder as he noticed she was on the verge of a panic attack. "Breathe, honey, she had it coming. She made her choice. It was going to come down to us or her in the end." Maeve shuddered, pushing aside the panic that threatened to overwhelm her. *No time for that now, Maeve.*

Mrs. Graham turned to Rachel while Trina began cleaning off the gore coating Mrs. Graham, attempting to return her to a semblance of her former self. "That sure was something…" Trina hesitated.

"Look, like Michael said, it was us or her. I know she was a person once, and I mourn the little girl she used to be. But she became something dark and twisted. We gave her a chance to go and live; she chose to double down on aiding a demon. She chose this path repeatedly. What's done is done. I'm not proud of it, but it was necessary."

While Trina wiped the carnage from Mrs. Graham, the older woman began to cry. "Rachel, I never gave up hope. My heart knew, but I refused to believe you were gone. I just… I'm so sorry."

Rachel planted a kiss that didn't quite land on her mother's cheek. "It's ok Mom. You didn't do anything wrong. All the fault lies with Dad and Scheana. What matters most is we're here, together. And you're going to put a stop to this."

While Mrs. Graham and Rachel carried on with their reunion, another family reunion began. Minerva approached Maeve and Michael, a smile splitting her face. "I'm so glad you two found one another. You will need all the power you can in order to take on Abaddon. He's waiting."

"Why hasn't he attacked yet, Mom? Why is he letting us waltz in?"

"We've been leading an uprising. The spirits have been tortured for centuries, but Abaddon made a mistake. Since he killed me at the seance, I was not bound to the lagoon. Bit by bit, I have done what I could. I rescued Celia first, and now Rachel. It's a hard task, but I have managed to free many who, in turn, freed others. They are still tied to the pit, but at least they are not in pain. My sisters have had hundreds of years to gather their anger. Abaddon thought he could cast us aside and slowly feed on our pain and suffering for eternity. He was woefully unprepared for a mass of women willing to take the fight to him. My sisters are numerous, with centuries of festering fury, and nothing to lose. With Celia leading them, they are fighting him as we speak, paving the way for you." Minerva paused, turning to Michael. "Michael, I...I'm so sorry."

"No apology needed, my love." He raised a hand, resting it near her face. "I will love you in this life and the next. You did what you had to do to protect our daughter."

Minerva smiled. "She's the best of us. I had eighteen years with her, it's your turn now. Please, protect her from what is to come." She turned to Maeve. "Our time grows short, sweetheart. Remember, you are more powerful than you realize. Only you can put an end to this. I love you and I am so immensely proud of you, Maeve."

"Thanks, Mom. I will break this curse, so no other women have to die." Minerva and Rachel smiled, then pulled away from the group, ushering them forward.

Minerva turned to Trina. "Thank you for being a lifelong friend. You shouldn't have had to clean up my messes...Michael, the Dickenson seance, Maeve. But you were always there. I couldn't have asked for a more loyal friend."

Trina smiled. "Of course. Friends stick together, even when one runs off and hides for eighteen years. You were always loved Minerva, even if it was from afar."

Minerva's voice turned solemn as she stood before the group one last time. "Come. It is time we take the fight to Abaddon."

Minerva and Rachel led the group as they steeled themselves for the fight ahead. Michael asked Maeve and Mrs. Graham, "Are we clear on the ritual? I will lead."

Maeve stared her dad down. "We are clear, but I will lead. He has feasted on the blood of women for centuries; it is only fitting that a woman end him."

Michael smirked. "I'm proud of you. I-" he cut off as the trees suddenly parted before them, revealing an otherworldly sight. A sea of ghostly women surrounded the lagoon and filled the air as they engaged in an all-out war with an array of demons. There were the hideous snakes and winged devils that the group had already encountered, but also numerous monstrosities they had yet to see. Abaddon truly had called forth the legions of Hell.

Empowered by Minerva breaking their hellish bonds, the women fought back against the horde. Celia led the charge, shouting orders as the women took the fight to the demons. Ichor coated the ground as demon after demon was cut down, centuries of rage released in furious retribution. As Abaddon yelled orders to his minions, Celia could be heard above the fray. "Arise my sisters! Let him feel our power! Daughters of Shady Grove, unite!"

Maeve watched in awe as Celia conjured a spear and threw it, hitting Abaddon in the wing. The demon screamed in pain and fury as he crashed toward the lagoon. Celia turned. "Join us, Maeve. The time for vengeance is now!" With her parents, the Graham women, and Trina behind her, Maeve confidently stepped into the fray.

Chapter Eighteen: Flames and Fury

Abaddon recovered at the last instant, the tip of his injured wing just grazing the fetid pool. The demons were distracted by the injury of their leader. Maeve pulled out her knife as the women parted for her, clearing a path to the edge of the lagoon. She saw women from various ages of history, recognizing pictures from NameUs: Amanda Corey, Tayla Whittmer, Antonia Roberts, Marie Weber. There were hundreds of all races, young and beautiful, their faces filled with righteous indignation.

As she made it to the edge, she noticed just how much progress the women had made. Countless demons were floating, dead by the women's hands, dragged back to Hell where they belonged. The screams of pain were no longer from Abaddon's victims but from his legions. Maeve took the knife and laid it against her palm. She sliced into the tender flesh, squeezing her blood into the lagoon.

"*Fovea desperationis, accipe sanguinem meum. De sanguine D'Arcy fluit per venas.*" The blood was pouring now as she sliced again, this time reopening the wound the previous demon had made to her shoulder. "*Separa nexum inter daemonem et hunc pagum-*" She cut off as a human scream filled the air. "Mrs. Graham!"

Abaddon had swooped down, grabbing Mrs. Graham in his clawed fist. The ghostly women renewed their attack as he took to the air. His voice boomed over the scene. "I normally don't accept sacrifices of such an advanced age, but I have hungered for you for years. Alain's newest wife, your daughter, was delicious. It is time to join her for eternity." He opened his hand, dropping Mrs. Graham into the lagoon.

"Mom!" Rachel flew across the surface, but try as she might, her hands could not grasp her mother's flailing form as she was pulled under the putrid ooze. Rachel sobbed as Mrs. Graham's head disappeared; yet another sacrifice to Abaddon. She flew into the air, howling with despair. "You will pay for this, Abaddon!" The demon swatted her from the air like a fly, sending her hurtling toward the earth.

Trina was in the fray of demons, her knives slicing through the air, felling all those in her way. Michael was behind her, protecting her despite his pain. Maeve had no choice but to continue the ritual as tears streamed down her face. *I'm sorry Mrs. Graham. You deserved so much better.* She stuck her arm in the lagoon, feeling the thick black substance begin to absorb her blood directly from her veins. *"Sanguis D'Arcy abrenuntiat-"*

"You will do no such thing, girl!" Abaddon raged, diving right for her.

"No!!!!" Trina dove, knocking Maeve out of the way. Abaddon's claws embedded in her chest, pulling forth her still-beating heart. His tail lashed through the air, skewering Michael through his leg.

"All who defy me will suffer eternal torment!" Trina slumped to the ground as the demon greedily devoured her heart. "Ah, such a pure soul. It is always such a pleasure to devour their lifeblood." Trina's blood dripped from Abaddon's wicked maw as he dove yet again. Maeve raised her hands, throwing holy water directly in his face. The demon screamed as he wrapped his hands around her and dove beneath the surface of the lagoon. The last thing Maeve heard as she was fully submerged was Michael desperately screaming her name.

She hurtled down, clutched in the demon's crushing grasp, for what felt like eternity. The heat was unbearable. She closed her eyes against the onslaught of pain assaulting her mind, body, and soul. Abaddon crashed into the ground, grinding her bones against sharp rock. *Where am I?* His grip relaxed and she opened her eyes, gasping against the pain. *Oh my god! Oh my god! OH MY GOD!*

Abaddon stood, unfurling his wings to their full glory. "Welcome to Hell, you obstinate woman!"

Maeve stood on aching, shaking legs. *Hey, I'm proud to be an obstinate woman!* Her feet struggled to gain purchase on the smooth obsidian beneath them as hellfire erupted all around them.

"You see, little girl, I wrote that grimoire. You really thought I would be stupid enough to include a ritual to banish me! You humans are so easily manipulated." *Of course! So stupid!* "Your mother may have unleashed the souls I held, but no one can free you down here. Your hubris blinded you to the truth. I am Abaddon the Destroyer. No power in Heaven nor Hell can defeat me.

Instead, you will be trapped here for eternity. As payment for your foolishness, you will be my broodmother, forced to birth me a new legion of demons. They will devour you from the inside, but I shall restore your body again and again, until you have replaced every demon your little friends have slain, tenfold. Welcome, Maeve, Mother of Demons."

Abaddon snapped his fingers. Iron chains clamped around Maeve, her body suddenly manacled to a slab of obsidian. Her eyes filled with horror as her stomach began to bulge and writhe, black shapes moving under the surface of the stretched skin. Abaddon sneered as she wept. "I should have mentioned, the process of growing a demon is...excruciating. This is your eternity." Maeve bent her head, screaming and weeping, as the claws of an unborn demon shredded her insides.

Back on the surface, the fierce battle continued. The ghostly women gained against the demon army, invigorated by Abaddon's retreat. But Michael and Minerva were in a flurry of panic. "He took her Michael! He took her to Hell!"

"How do we get to her? We have to help her! FUCK!"

"I don't know if my spirit can survive another trip down into the depths. Each time, you lose a bit of your soul. I freed so many of these women," Minerva gestured at the souls around them, "but I have no choice. He has Maeve. Maybe he will accept my soul in exchange for hers."

"Let me come with you."

"Michael, to go to Hell, you would have to be dead."

"Better dead than leaving the two greatest loves of my life to suffer in Hell. Plus, if our estimations are right, this sting" he gestured at his leg, "will kill me in nine months, anyway. And it will be slow and agonizing, like poor Ed Dickenson." With that, Michael slit his wrists and waded into the lagoon. The pool greedily devoured the offered blood. Michael closed his eyes, relishing the exquisite pain. When he opened them, he was floating above his body, Minerva extending her hand to him.

"Are you ready to fight a demon for the soul of our daughter?"

As he died, he felt Minerva grab his hand. Michael was overjoyed to be reunited, even if it was in death. "Let's go, my love."

Chapter Nineteen: Obsidian and Blood

Maeve screamed as the first claw tore through her skin, followed by a vicious bite. She knew she was bleeding internally, yet was powerless to stop it. Her body ached with every breath as the demon tore her to shreds, just as Abaddon promised. Her blood made the obsidian slab slick as she writhed, but the chains held her steady. There was no escape from the pain, the birth, the torment. Abaddon traced a claw down her face, drawing blood as he went.

"I told you, you will birth my army. Humans and demons alike will revile you." He spat in her face, the foul substance clouding her vision and catching in her throat. *I. Can't. Take. Much. More.*

The blood-soaked demon burst from her stomach, leaving her screaming in pain. Blood poured out upon the slab, relentless in its pursuit to be free of her body. Her heartbeat grew weaker. Her breaths came in shuddering gasps. She closed her eyes...and then Abaddon snapped his fingers.

For a brief moment, Maeve felt reborn. She was no longer covered in blood, her body split over the hellscape that surrounded her. But her relief was short-lived. Abaddon smiled his twisted grin. "Good...now again. We're just getting started." With a snap of his claws, Maeve felt the now familiar twisting sensation of a demon spawn deep within her gut. She screamed as Abaddon let loose another bout of hideous laughter.

Minerva and Michael burst through the portal, their bodies restored amongst the hellscape. "The better to torture souls if they can feel physical pain," Michael whispered.

Minerva nodded. They took a moment to orient themselves before their eyes locked on their daughter in ruined bloody clothes, chained with infernal iron to a slab. Minerva's eyes blazed crimson with a fury that was only matched by Hell itself. She closed her eyes, letting her rage build until a weapon soaked in love and wrath materialized in her hands. As Maeve began to scream below her, Minerva heaved her flaming sword into Abaddon's neck.

Abaddon roared at the unexpected blow. He was so focused on relishing Maeve's suffering; he had not noticed the pair enter his domain uninvited. Michael flew to his daughter's side, hoping to find a way to ease Maeve's suffering. He grabbed her hand, offering his silent support as he assessed the situation.

"D-dad?"

"I'm here honey. Your mother and I are going to get you out of this!"

"It-it hur-ts so much D-dad..." her voice shook, dissolving into screams as the demon inside her began to fight its way out. Michael could only watch in horror as Maeve was torn apart from the inside. "DAD!!!"

Minerva heaved her sword a second time, prepared to wage war against Abaddon. The glint in his eye stopped her. "You realize I am the only thing keeping your daughter alive." She watched in blind panic as the demon spawn clawed its way out of Maeve with more brutality than the first. Michael held her hand helplessly as she died. With a snap of his fingers, Abaddon brought her back. He held off on the second snap, letting Michael and Minerva see the power he held.

Minerva lowered her sword, grasping the futility of the situation. Michael bowed his head and wept, his tears mingling with Maeve's as she awaited the next round of torture. "What...what will it take to end this?" Michael whispered.

"To end what, exactly?"

Michael opened his mouth to speak, but Minerva cut in. "To return our daughter, alive and unharmed, to the human realm. To end the D'Arcy bloodline curse. And to end the hold the lagoon has on Shady Grove?"

"Ahhhhh....I see you know to be very precise when dealing with demons." Abaddon hesitated, licking his lips in anticipation. "I am, after all, a bargaining soul. I will meet your demands, one soul for each condition. Minerva, you will take your daughter's place, birthing demons until the end of time itself. Michael, you will burn in the lake of fire, watching Minerva birth my spawn, but helpless to aid her..."

Minerva flew to her daughter, kissing her on the head. "My soul for hers, correct? If I take her place, you will return her, alive and unharmed, to the human realm?"

"Yes, your soul for hers."

Michael held tightly to Maeve as the family wept. "And as for me, which deal will my soul's torment fulfill?"

"Your soul, Michael, will release the curse on the D'Arcy line. I will no longer require sacrifices from your bloodline."

Minerva returned her watery gaze to Abaddon. "You mentioned a third soul? How do we know if we agree you simply won't return to drag Maeve back down here?"

The demon's maw spread into a wicked, twisted grin. "Ahhh, I thought you would never ask. You see, there is one soul I seek above all others, but our deal prevents me from doing him direct harm. He has centuries of death on his hands. If I return Maeve, she must sacrifice Alain D'Arcy to the pit. Upon acquiring his soul, I will break my bond with Shady Grove. Do we have a deal?"

Minerva kissed Maeve again, whispering softly, "I love you, sweetheart, never forget that." Turning to Abaddon, her voice rang out with a mother's undying love. "Release my daughter, demon, and I will accept your deal." At once, Maeve was released from the slab. Michael pulled her up as her body shook.

Maeve screamed as Minerva laid down willingly on the slab, the chains attaching themselves to her gleefully. Abaddon snapped his fingers, and Minerva joined in the screaming. Michael bowed his head, pulling Maeve in for a tight embrace.

"Our time together was too short, but I would say that even if we had had a lifetime together. I love you Maeve, and it was an honor to be your dad, even if only for a few days."

Michael released his daughter and declared to Abaddon, "I also accept my fate in order to clear my bloodline of this wretched curse." Abaddon grinned. He grabbed Michael and threw him into the fiery lake. Michael's spirit immediately caught fire, and he writhed in agony.

"What a tragedy. The young lovers, together forever yet always apart. I will relish your pain for all of eternity." Abaddon cackled, his laugh shaking the very bowels of Hell. "Alas, I must uphold my end of the bargain." With that, Abaddon reached out and grabbed a weeping Maeve, crushing her in his grasp as he hurtled out of Hell, back through the surface of the lagoon.

Chapter Twenty: A Soul for A Soul

Abaddon did as he promised, returning Maeve to the surface. The battle still raged, but it was obvious the women were winning. The lagoon was littered with the carcasses of deceased demons, their ichor melding seamlessly with the vile ooze. He placed Maeve on the bank, in the exact spot where he had originally snatched her.

"Girl, bring me the soul of Alain D'Arcy. Or this war will continue for eternity. As a sign of my goodwill, I have returned the souls of your beloved Trina and Mrs. Graham to the surface. They will fight me until you end this, girl."

Tears streaming down her face, Maeve nodded. Her heart ached with the knowledge that her parents had damned themselves to eternal torment to save her. *How do I live with myself after this?* But another still small voice replied, *Make them proud.* Maeve gritted her teeth, her body aching. It had been restored, yet still reeled from the two demonic births she endured. *Alain, you bastard, it's time to pay up.*

Maeve stalked through the woods, using Celia's glowing markers in reverse as a way to keep on track. The solo journey was somber. *Mom. Dad. Trina. Mrs. Graham. Rachel.* All dead by Abaddon's doing, all stuck in an eternal war only she could end. Finally, the sound of low groaning met her ears.

Maeve stalked into the clearing, no longer afraid of anything lurking in the woods. She had gone to Hell and back, losing everyone she loved in the process. She had nothing left, but she could still save her ancestral home. Smirking, she towered over Alain's ruined, crumpled form. "Hello, Alain."

Alain D'Arcy stared back, hate evident in his glare. "You bitch!" he screamed, spit flying from his mouth.

Maeve glared right back, unintimidated. "Abaddon requires your soul, and it will be my pleasure to deliver it."

Two demons appeared as Abaddon's voice rang out, "I sent your children to help you. Use them wisely."

Alain's countenance fell at Abaddon's words. "Your...your...children?"

Maeve ignored the question. "You condemned me to Hell! Abaddon struck a deal, your soul in exchange for all of this to be over. I have no problem serving you up to Hell on a platter. You deserve nothing less." She clapped her hands, and the demons grabbed Alain, their sharp claws digging into his underarms as they dragged him to the lagoon, blood from his ruined knees marking the ground as they went.

Alain screamed the entire way, as the demon's claws soaked with his blood. His ruined knees screamed with every bounce, which the demons gleefully caused. *Serves you right, this is all your fault. All this death, and for what?* Finally, they reached the edge of the pool. A woman, clothed in a long, flowing night shift came forward. "Alain?" she gasped.

Alain D'Arcy hung his head in shame as he stared into the eyes of his long-lost Lizbet. "Was it worth it Alain?"

"No," he groveled. "I always regretted losing you. I lied to myself. Said I did it for the town, that I didn't care.

But I have missed you every day, my love." Lizbet spat in his face.

"Liar! I don't believe a word out of your wretched mouth. Rot. In. Hell." The women gathered around as Maeve and her demon accomplices brought Alain to the edge of the lagoon. Tears stung Maeve's eyes as she recognized the battle-weary faces of Trina, Mrs. Graham, Rachel, and Celia. Even in death, they led the charge against Abaddon. They, more than almost anyone, deserved to witness this.

Alain grew desperate, his eyes wide with fear at what awaited him. "Please! Please, no! There has to be another way! Anything, please!"

Maeve shoved the man into the mire, flanked by her demon spawn, as she solemnly watched Alain D'Arcy drown in the pool anchored by his own wretched deeds. He thrashed, the force of his flailing causing waves to disturb the surface, but to no avail. He screamed until the thick liquid flooded his throat, drowning him as he sank beneath the surface, down into the depths of Hell.

"There is no mercy for the likes of you, Alain D'Arcy."

The ground began to shake, knocking Maeve to the ground. "What the?" The forest quaked as the ground split, the lagoon seeping down into the cracks. The shaking slowly subsided, and as Maeve stood, she came to a startling realization. She was alone. The lagoon was gone, just as Abaddon had promised. The silence was deafening. Maeve could only assume the souls of the women had been released and the demons had returned to Hell with their master.

Maeve looked around. There was one last thing she had to do. Finally, her eyes landed on an unmoving form under one of the beech trees. She ran over, hoping she wasn't too late. On the ground, bound and gagged, was the sleeping form of McKinley Summers. Maeve gently shook the girl awake as she freed her from her bonds. "Shhhh... Shhhh, I'm here to help."

McKinley cried when she saw Maeve. Her throat sounded horribly parched. "Are you, are you with them?"

"No, McKinley, they're gone. Let's get you home." Together the two girls walked through the forest, Maeve guided by Celia's now fading sigils. It took almost two hours, but when they finally breached the treeline out of the forest, both girls stood in shock. Shady Grove had been hit by an earthquake. McKinley fell to the ground with exhaustion.

"Please, find help."

"I'll be back soon." Maeve jogged into Shady Grove, taking in the devastation as she went. The townspeople were out and about, sifting through the rubble of destroyed buildings, hoping to save those trapped within. Firefighters joined in the rescue efforts, while EMTs treated anyone who was injured. Several people simply stood in shock. Maeve stumbled as she found what she could only assume had been the epicenter of the destruction, a giant sinkhole where the Graham's house once stood. Her heart leaped into her throat. *So many innocent lives gone...so much destruction.* Finally, her eyes landed on a pair of police officers.

"Help!" she cried, struggling to be heard over the hub of activity around her. "Help, please! I found McKinley Summers, but she's hurt!" *THAT got their attention.* Maeve was swarmed by police and medical personnel as she led the way to McKinley. The injured girl was whisked away in an ambulance while two police officers stayed to ask Maeve some questions.

"My name is Officer Huddle, and this is my partner, Officer Schultz. How did you find McKinley Summers?"

Maeve's mind whirled. She didn't want to lie, but she also couldn't exactly tell the officers she had gone off into the forest to stop a demon and break a curse. "I saw Ronald Graham go off into the forest, acting suspicious. I went after him with..." Her heart clenched as the reality of all she had lost set in. "With Trina and Michael from the bookshop. We followed him out there, but then the earthquake hit. It...It..."

The female officer placed her hand gently on Maeve's shoulder. "Deep breaths. It's ok now, you're safe. When you're ready, just tell us what happened."

Maeve nodded, focusing on her breathing as she narrowly avoided a full-blown panic attack. *I'm going to need therapy for the rest of my life after this.* "We found McKinley and an accomplice of Mr. Graham. But the earthquake, it just...it swallowed them. Only McKinley and I made it out. Everyone else is...gone." Her voice trembled on the last syllable as Maeve burst into tears. Officer Huddle embraced Maeve, her stalwart presence comforting the young woman.

Officer Shultz coughed. "I'm sorry to break this up, but we need to head to the hospital to talk to Ms. Summers and her family. Will you be around, Miss..." he trailed off, realizing in their haste for answers, they had forgotten to even get her name.

"Maeve, Maeve Baudelaire. Michael was my father. I'll be staying in Shady Grove." She looked around, once again feeling her heart break with both the town's destruction and her personal losses. "I'll be around." The officers nodded, grabbing Maeve's contact information before heading to the hospital.

Maeve squared her shoulders as she headed toward the ruins of Trina's Trinkets and Tomes, sirens wailing through the town and people screaming. But amidst the chaos, there was also hope. People worked side by side, doing whatever they could to help their neighbors. *I am Maeve Baudelaire, the last D'Arcy. I am a survivor. Together, Shady Grove and I will rebuild.* Smiling faintly, she got to work. Among the remains of Trina's store, she found something. Miraculously untouched lay Trina's ouija board and planchette. Her fingers sparked as they grazed the wood, tingling with power. Maeve felt Trina smiling down upon her as her spiritual gifts fully awakened. *Message received, Trina. I'll be in touch. Mom, Dad...hold on. I'm coming back for you. Hoc non est super, Abaddon. This isn't over.*

THE END

Acknowledgements

This book would not be possible without a myriad of people rallying around me with unconditional love and support. First and foremost, I want to thank my husband, Adam, for being my number one supporter. He read this manuscript more than my editor, every single draft, multiple times...and he's not even a horror reader. My mom, for passing on her love of horror, and for inspiring the character of Mrs. Graham with her heart and her delicious cooking. For anyone concerned, Mr. Graham is not inspired by my dad, who is also a lovely human being. And my daughters, who are my inspiration for everything. Girls, Mommy wrote a book!

There were so many people behind the scenes helping me with this book that it is unreal. Gage Greenwood, for being a mentor and helping me connect with some of the best bookish friends in the world. I love both the cult and the Scribes. The Chaos Scribes are an infinite source of encouragement, patience, and fun! Stephanie Huddle, for being the most patient, badass editor. Jyl Glenn, for helping me figure out formatting and the world of publishing, as well as being my first Patreon subscriber. Jennifer Kelly-Watt, for endless entertainment and David Cassidy's balls. To my beta readers: Dylan Wells, Charlotte Stevenson, Sally Feliz, Molly Mix, Eve L. Fell, Glenda Starr, Beverly Laude, Barry Hollywood, and Jasmin Hoffman. Without these people behind me, Incantations of Blood wouldn't exist. Thank you everyone.

About the Author

Savannah R. Fischer is the permanently exhausted pigeon in charge of two well-loved chaos gremlins. When not with her family, she can usually be found in her horror den, wrapped in an oversized blanket and dreaming of spinach puffs. She wants to show her gremlins that they can do hard things, even when it's scary, like pulling the wrong lever and ending up in a pit of alligators. No llamas were harmed in the making of her works of horror.

About the Editor

Stephanie Huddle is a college professor who teaches her students about real-life human horrors and spends countless hours reading and grading papers. She works so she can afford to give her cats the lifestyle they have come to expect. She has been an avid reader since childhood, and while her go-to genre is horror, she also likes fantasy, thriller, and sci-fi. When she's not reading for work or leisure, Stephanie enjoys watching true crime documentaries, horror movies, and anything weird. She also spends more time than she should wondering why she even has that lever. She can be reached at sh.editing1408@gmail.com

Follow Along Here

Like what you read? Follow my journey on social media to keep up with the latest updates on upcoming works! My Patreon also features work in progress updates, behind the scenes of the stories, and free monthly short stories.

Facebook: Savannah R. Fischer

Instagram: @s.r.fischerauthor

TikTok: @s.r.fischerauthor

Patreon: Savannah R. Fischer's Penguin Posse

Recommended Reading

If you enjoyed Incantations of Blood, I highly recommend the following titles from other indie authors killing the horror genre.

It Eats Your Hunger by Joseph Murnane

The Willows by K.L. Allister

The Considerate Cannibal by Kimberly Nicole

Fiery Mable by Kristal Shanahan

It Came From the Pumpkin Patch by Chris Heinicke & Kate Reedwood

Season of the Monster Series by AJ Humphreys

Blood Brawl by Derek Thomas

In The Eyes, In The Shadows by Gage Greenwood

Impulse by Megan Stockton

Duncan Ralston is Dead by Lisa Breanne

Gollitok by Andrew Najberg

Cadaverous by Jay Bower

The Cursed Among Us by John Durgin

The Darkle Chronicles by B.C. Hollywood

The Namaste Slasher by Alan Shivers

The Dark Thing by John Ashley